'Cra

RedSox
Press

Published by RedSox Press 2018
www.redsoxpress.co.uk

ISBN 978-1-9995809-5-7

RedSox Press Limited Reg. No. 09863441

Typeset by RedSox Press UK

Printed by CreateSpace

CRASH!

By

J. M. Hulme

Beginnings

'Every new beginning comes from some other
beginnings end'

Lucius Annaeus Seneca

For
Wendy and Sally
my amazing daughters—always there for me.

Prologue

It began as a pretty unspectacular morning. Claustrophobic, dark clouds hung heavily overhead, the wet roads reflecting their gloomy greyness.

Frowning people, rushing to their places of work, their heads down and their brollies up obscuring their vision, could be seen manoeuvring around the many puddles which were growing upon the pavements and along the gutters. Rain dripped down their collars and ran cold onto their exposed necks, soaking into their clothes and adding to their soggy discomfort. Cars passed by in hearse-like procession, the slushing sound of their tyres creating a monotonous musical beat to accompany the roar of their engines. Drivers could be seen sitting tense as they peered through misted windows, their windscreen wipers waving their arms in time to the dirge-like overture. It was just another typical Monday morning—a scene played out in cities everywhere—but today, for some, it was to be a day that would change their lives forever.

Tessa Matthews was sitting, staring at the bare walls of her classroom while waiting for her new intake class to arrive at the beginning of a new school year.

One of the children she waited for was Daisy, who was also staring ahead; far too nervous about her first day at her new school to worry about what was going on around her. She was more concerned with how she would find her way around the unfamiliar building than she was with her journey.

Danny Stokes was feeling anxious for a different reason. The butterflies whirling around in his stomach were caused by the thought of seeing the lovely Lucinda again!

Lucinda's chauffeur on this wretchedly wet and miserable Monday morning was her father, Brendon Green. He thought himself a pillar of society. He was a man whose sole purpose in life was to make people admire him.

Mary Parsons, however, didn't care a toss about what people thought of her. She was just agitated by the volume of traffic and the careless drivers who were delaying her arrival at work, where she was obliged to conduct a job interview—and she certainly wasn't contemplating being late for anyone!

Frank was possibly the only person that wasn't anxious this morning! He hadn't a care in the world as he jogged his way to work in the heavy rain—the weather being the last thing to upset this energetic man!

Valerie was feeling far from energetic after the night she had had! Her feelings were more of guilt. Guilt about the affair she was having with her boss—and the hope that she would arrive home before her poor unsuspecting husband could question where she'd been.

Lastly, there was Alan, once again fuming, as he was most mornings, because the 8.05 bus was late yet again!

Little did they all know on this miserable Monday morning how much their lives would soon be altered—by just one careless moment!

Tess
Chapter 1

Tessa Matthews walked down the long windowless corridor, feeling the pale green walls rearing up on either side of her. She took in the dark smudges, where many grubby hands had made their marks, and many shoes had scuffed. It reminded her of some poor trapped soul trying to kick and claw their way out.

The bare, windowless doors along the left-hand side also painted green, but of a darker shade, showed at least some thought had gone into its interior design. Each door had a keypad—a stark reminder visitors were not to be welcomed. The centre of each door held a number plate, no names, just numbers here!

The corridor stretched before her, brown and bare, encouraging the sound of her footsteps to bounce off the walls and echo as she walked on. She rounded the corner and the same infinite scene went on before her, same walls, same doors, same keypads, only the number plates were different.

Fire-doors blocked her way, displaying another keypad, so she punched in a code. The doors reluctantly opened to allow her to pass, before quickly closing again, like a Venus fly trap capturing its unsuspecting victim.

A narrow staircase leading down beckoned her and with heavy tread she descended into the bowels of the building, once again wondering if hell would be quite so unwelcoming. After another corridor, exactly like those that had come before, she reached her destination. She stood in front of the green door, like all the other green doors, except for its distinguishing number and she punched in its exclusive four digits. At first, it was, as usual, unwilling to accept her code but after repeating the process once more, it found its target and with an ominous click the door opened, issuing a throaty groan as it croaked its evil greeting, its weight trying to push against her to stop her passage.

With her foot acting as a wedge to keep the door open, she eased the large bag she was carrying in through the small gap and, with sneering, mocking laughter the door slowly swung back, locking her inside her tomb for the day.

She flicked the switch on the wall and waited while the fluorescent light flickered several times before finally bursting into life. The room was stark, just a large brown wooden keyhole desk, with drawers either side— locked of course. Three piles of chairs were stacked in mounds of eight behind the desk. This was where she was supposed to make the magic happen! This was where unquestioning students would soon arrive to gain their knowledge.

In this quiet time before their arrival, it seemed impossible to think this hell-hole would soon come to life and the green walls would ring with the sound of chatter and laughter, and the room vibrate with joy! Soon knowledge would be absorbed, and it would all be worthwhile—but each time she came here at this hour in the morning, before the walls had woken to begin their day, she felt the knot begin to tighten in her stomach. She had to make it happen! It was her obligation to those who would soon enter. They also had to tread those hostile corridors! It was her duty to dispel their feelings of hopelessness, dispel the feeling she felt each time she made her way down to this room. It was her duty to make the magic occur. So she sat and watched the walls as she waited for their arrival, and very slowly the school began to come to life.

A new term, a new school year, but this one was to be different from all the others.

Daisy
Chapter 2

'It isn't fair—why did I have to come to this poxy school! Why couldn't I go to the same school as my friends? Why did we have to move just because of Gran?'

There were so many questions whizzing around inside Daisy's head; questions she'd asked her mother over and over again without getting a satisfactory reply.

Now, here she was on her way, and there wasn't a thing she could do about it. Her stomach was churning so much she thought she'd throw up at any moment. It was so hard leaving her old life behind, the life where she knew all the teachers so well, and even though she had little to do with the other girls, they at least had familiar faces. That school had been small, not like the monstrosity she was heading for now! She wouldn't know anyone here. No familiar faces—no one to help her find her way. She could visualise her old friends now; all gathered together, all helping each other to get settled in. They would arrange to meet up at playtime—who would she talk to? She wouldn't know a soul, no one would join her in. She was sure she'd get lost and everyone would laugh at her and watch her from afar and whisper.

She looked once more into the sun visor mirror of her mother's car and for the umpteenth time rearranged her hair.

'I hate my hair like this! Why did you make me have it cut so short? I look like a boy!' she exclaimed to her mother, 'and just look at these sleeves! This blazer is far too big for me! I'll be a laughing stock!' On the verge of tears Daisy pushed back the mirror into its housing and with a deep sigh got out her mobile phone

'No texts. There isn't anyone that bothers enough to wish me luck. I bet they're all texting each other though. They won't miss me. Who cares if that quiet little mouse in the corner has had to leave?'

'You look lovely darling, don't worry so much. You'll be dressed exactly the same as everyone else, so stop fretting!' Daisy's mother glanced across at her disgruntled daughter and although concerned by her obvious misery, she tried hard not to allow it to show. She knew Daisy had been unhappy about the move, but what else could she do, when her ailing mother needed her!

'Ah look, we're here now!' She turned the car left between the big gates that led down the school drive towards the carpark. Daisy reluctantly dragged her eyes away from her phone and looked up. The sight before her made her take in breath.

In front of her was the most amazing house she had ever seen! Although she'd been here before it now looked quite different. It had been dark the last time she'd seen it, when she'd attended the new pupil intake meeting with her mother—and she hadn't taken much notice then anyway, as she thought she'd be going to the same school as her friends! She didn't realise her mother had been serious about moving—that she'd already bought a new house, so they'd be living nearer to Granny, and that she'd have to make new friends!

This school now in front of her was grand and imposing! It looked like one of those stately homes she was often dragged around during the school holidays. Even on this dark and dreary morning Daisy was spellbound. Rain glistened on the two stone pillars either side of the entrance, both of which encased a statue. They reminded her of Knights in shining armour, placed there to protect her from the world.

They drove through the enormous iron gates, following the road that led them down a tree lined drive. The school building stood regally in front of them. The road then veered off to the right as Daisy's mother followed the signs to the car park. Once the car had come to a halt Daisy switched off her mobile phone and dropped it inside her school bag. She then did up its straps, before taking a deep breath—this was now the time for her to be brave and to leave her mum!

'Don't make a fuss Mum, and please don't kiss me or the other kids will see! Yes I've got everything I need!

See you tonight.' Turning her face away from her mother she got quickly out of the car, not daring to look back, she knew she'd cry if she did.

She followed the other girls, who all seemed to know each other, over to the front of the building, where a stone staircase rose up in front of imposing, crest emblazoned, entrance doors.

Now was the time for make-believe.

'I can get by if I pretend to be someone else,' she told herself.

Suddenly her mind took over, and her short fair hair was now long and flowing down her back. Her school uniform had magically disappeared and in its place was the most beautiful long gown of golden silk, which was fitted at the waist and had a row of tiny hand embroidered buttons running down the front of the bodice. The neck was edged with the finest lace. In her mind, she'd transported herself back to the eighteenth century!

With her head held high, she took each step carefully and gracefully. She breathed in and out slowly and deeply, and as she did so, a feeling of calm command entered her body. When she reached the top of the steps, she turned to look back along the driveway. She saw its manicured lawns on either side, and she smiled as she visualised a coach, pulled by two sleek black horses, coming down the drive towards her.

Daisy turned and walked slowly into the grand building, where she looked up at high ceilings, elaborately carved and edged with patterned cornices. Instead of the school, which was now buzzing with lively pupils greeting each other warmly after their long summer vacation, she saw maids and butlers busily going about their duties, making everything ready for her arrival.

A bell rang somewhere in the distance.

'They must be summoning for someone to come and greet me,' she thought.

Oh, how she loved it here! It was so grand! She belonged here! Never again would she worry about her blazer and her short unruly hair because she knew, from that day on, whatever happened, she could always recall wearing her beautiful gown of golden silk—or of deep blue velvet when it was really cold—and no one would ever know but her.

Daisy never did tell anyone, but from that day on— the day when her nightmare began and her whole world fell apart and was turned upside down—in her darkest moments she would remember this place and would once again reach back into her memory to the moment she had learnt to use her magic and transform herself from a chrysalis into a beautiful butterfly—and her imagination would take her again down the long driveway, where she would see the approaching black horses, and remember once more becoming an elegant young lady dressed in gold.

What she didn't foresee was how soon her nightmare was going to happen and how, before long; she'd find herself completely lost and alone. On this bleak September morning, she would realise how temporary life is and how foolish she'd been to think moving to a new school was the end of her world. This was the day when twelve-year-old Daisy was forced to grow up, the day she learnt what it was like to be really on her own.

Danny
Chapter 3

Danny Stokes was nearly eighteen—at least he would be very soon. He'd finally managed to persuade his parents to let him have a party, and so he should have felt excited. However, this morning all he felt was confused and angry. He peered; frowning into the hall mirror, checking to make sure every hair on his head was in place before he left his house ready to face the world. His appearance was important to him. Looking good gave him confidence.

'Bye Mum', he shouted from the hallway.

His mother appeared at the top of the stairs, looking immaculate as usual, struggling to put on the jacket of her grey trouser suit. Jennifer Stokes, a partner in a law firm in the city, shouted back down the stairs to her son.

'Bye darling! Don't forget I have to work late again tonight, so you'll have to let yourself in and get your own tea. I've left a lasagne in the fridge for you to pop in the microwave.' She blew him a goodbye kiss.

'Yes Mum, you told me all that last night!' Danny replied, smiling as he returned the kiss. 'How long is Dad's business trip likely to last this time?'

'He's not sure darling. He thinks it could be a couple of weeks, but that'll depend if his work schedule goes according to plan! Have you got your key?'

'Yes Mum.' He dangled his key in the air to show her.

'Did you pick up your dinner money? I left it on the kitchen table!'

'Yes Mum!'

'Have a good first day back at school darling! I'll see you later this evening.'

'OK, I will!' He opened the front door and let himself out into the pouring rain. 'Oh great, that's all I need,' he thought as he pulled up the hood of his anorak. 'What's the point of spending hours on my hair in this weather?' He put in his headphones and turned up the music. Music always made him feel brighter, helped him to forget the teenage problems which weighed so heavily on his young shoulders this morning.

Danny was a very handsome young man, tall and slim, with jet black hair. His dark, swarthy, Mediterranean features had been inherited from his Italian grandmother. He came from a loving family, and although they were not always there for him, he realised it was only because they worked so hard that he was able to have all the material things he required. He always had the newest gadgets, latest clothes, most expensive trainers—in fact he was every young girls dream.

11

He exuded an air of confidence, walked with a fashionable swagger and could sometimes appear to be a bit of a show-off. However, that was only the face he presented to the world, a 'Jack the Lad' image, designed to create the impression he was someone who wasn't afraid to speak out and to be heard. At heart he was less confident, using all the clothes, gadgets and so forth, to give himself greater street cred, which he needed more than ever this morning to build his flagging ego. He was popular right enough, never without friends, but never anyone close, never anyone special. He seemed afraid to get too closely involved with anyone in case he might get hurt. Yet deep down inside, stability was the one thing he craved most of all.

True he'd snogged Amy Sanders behind the bicycle shed when he was fifteen but who hadn't! It was all part of growing up—and Amy was ever ready to oblige. Later the said Amy, who had progressed and become more experienced in the art, suddenly left school halfway through a term and although there was much speculation about her equally sudden weight gain, no one was ever told exactly why she'd left or where she'd gone. They could only listen to rumours and gossip about who the prospective father might be. Danny had his suspicions that a red-haired boy with acne called Billy Brewer seemed to be the most likely candidate.

If anyone cared enough to look beyond Danny's boasting and bravado, they'd find there lay a very insecure and sensitive young man. A young man who spent much of his life pushing himself forward to achieve the goals his parents, particularly his Dad, expected of him.

His father was a well-known politician, who was most often away working. Danny often wished he belonged to an ordinary family, with a nine till five Dad and a mother who was waiting for him when he arrived home from school, with a welcoming biscuit and a hot drink, ready to listen to his ramblings about his mundane day. How he hated going into an empty house! How he dreaded the quiet. The first thing he always did when he got home from school was to put on the television, not because he wanted to sit and watch it but because it helped to disguise the loneliness and the silence.

However, he was also aware, as he had been told so many times, that the empty house wouldn't be quite so comfortable to come home to if they didn't both go out work, neither would he have all the trappings that went along with it.

He couldn't fault his parents. When they were there they were both loving and caring—all he craved was their attention sometimes, instead of seeing them with their heads stuck in books or working for hours on their computers. Any conversations he had with them were usually serious and thought provoking. Danny just wished they'd lighten up occasionally. How he longed to hear them laugh about silly, inconsequential things. How he wished they'd watch tele as a normal family did together! As he walked to school in the pouring rain he mulled over this, feeling hard done by. Once again, he'd have to go home to an empty house, there'd be no one there waiting for him to offload his current problem.

'I suppose they'd only tell me I'm too young to be serious about a girl,' he thought. 'Well, perhaps they'd be right. Perhaps I shouldn't get serious about anyone for a while yet, not at my age! Maybe I need to play the field first, make sure I take advantage of what life has on offer for me, without the added pressure of a girlfriend. There are loads of things I intend to try before I settle down! I certainly don't want to end up like Billy Brewer with a kid before I leave school! I'm going to university; I need to get some qualifications and a good job behind me before I get serious about any girl! You only get hurt if you let them in anyway—and I can do without that! Oh, why are girls so complicated? Yes! I intend to play the field for a good few years yet before I let myself in for a kid and a mortgage!'

With his future sorted he took out his mobile phone and looked at his messages.

'I wonder why she hasn't messaged me back though. Perhaps she doesn't fancy me after all. Perhaps the smile she gave me when I bumped into her in town yesterday was just a tease. Maybe I read too much into it. Oh, why did I have to go and send her that stupid text last night? I bet she thinks I'm a right loser now! Well, it's her loss if she doesn't want to come to my party, to hell with her! I managed without her before, and I can darn well do the same thing again!' With that he picked up his pace and marched purposefully on, oblivious to the fact his life was soon to be turned suddenly upon its head!

Mary
Chapter 4

Peering through the misted, rain-streaked window of her Ford Fiesta, Mary sat watching her windscreen wipers going to and fro. She waited impatiently for the traffic lights to change to green and the sluggish driver in front of her to get going! As she sat there, fingers drumming on the steering wheel, she pondered about the interview she'd be holding later that morning and thought over the questions she'd need to ask. She'd interviewed so many young hopefuls for this post already but until now that is what they remained— hopeful! No one had seemed quite up to the mark.

She tutted and shook her head.

'Young folk these days have no commitment. They'd rather sponge off their parents than knuckle down and get a career.'

A horn blared from somewhere behind her, and she realised the lights had changed to green.

'Keep your hair on, it's not my fault!' she yelled to whoever may have been listening. 'If you're in such a hurry try telling the woman in the 4x4 in front! I don't think she's ever experienced bad weather driving before!'

Mary sounded her horn to alert the driver in front to get going.

Once the said woman had begun to move, Mary quickly put her car through its gears and continued on her journey. She caught up once more with the sluggish morning traffic, and her mind drifted back to work and to her own interview years before, when she'd first joined the company. She could visualise herself now, as clear as if it were only yesterday, wearing a navy-blue suit, the one she kept specially for such occasions. She was sitting nervously outside the interview room. She bit her bottom lip as she remembered the sinking feeling she'd experienced that day and recalled her sweaty, shaking hands. She frowned as she experienced once again the sense of hopelessness she'd felt, as the interviewee before her came out of the room; a perfect size eight, with perfectly applied makeup and immaculately coiffured hair!

As she cast her mind back, she could remember thinking to herself 'Well, that's the end of that then! No doubt Miss Anorexia will get the job! I doubt they'll want a big fat cow like me cluttering up their perfect little office!' She could vaguely recall thinking she needed to lose weight if she wanted to get a decent job, but then smiled as she remembered dismissing the thought out of hand because she knew it would be far too difficult for her to accomplish.

'So what if I do like my food too much?' she asked the steering wheel. 'That's my problem and no one

17

else's. If people can't see beyond my size, then the problem is theirs!'

How she'd hated being judged by how she looked. No one had ever taken her seriously because of her size. How it angered her that people were so insular, so short-sighted. They'd never given her the chance to prove herself. She knew she could have done most of the jobs she'd applied for standing on her head, far better than the stick insects that spent most of their day looking into a mirror! If only someone had given her a chance and allowed her to try. She smiled now as the image of her standing on her head entered her mind.

'Just because I don't look like Cheryl Cole, or whatever she calls herself these days, doesn't mean I'm stupid,' she voiced loudly to a woman who ran across the road in front of her. 'Unlike you, you silly old fool! What do you think they put zebra crossings across the road for—zebras?'

Mary had suffered a weight problem all her life. At school, it meant it wasn't cool to be seen sitting next to her, which in turn meant she'd been isolated and had no friends.

'It's not been easy being me,' she thought, 'If only folk knew how many times I've tried to diet! If only they knew how hard it is. It's a vicious circle. If you're fat nobody wants you, so you sit in alone each night. That's when you reach out for the chocolate box! What else have you got to enjoy?'

Her mind panned back to the sultry female voice on the intercom calling her into the interview room and she let out a deep sigh as she remembered thinking, 'Well here goes!' She shook her head and chuckled inwardly as she visualised releasing herself from the chair in which she'd become wedged, before half-heartedly walking over to the interview room door. 'No doubt this would be just another wasted journey!' She chuckled, this time loudly, at the memory of thinking, 'If I don't get this job I'm going straight round to the doctor to get a gastric band fitted and to hell with the cost!'

Another horn, or possibly even the same impatient commuter, blared from somewhere behind her, dragging her back into reality as she pulled up yet again behind the silver Range Rover. She seethed inside as she found herself in another traffic jam and reached over to open the glove compartment to take out a Mars Bar, which she felt might console her.

'Why are the roads all so damn busy this morning!' she brooded. 'No doubt it's because all the mummies and daddies are out taking their little brats to school in case the little darlings should get slightly wet! Well don't bother about us real workers will you!' she shouted as she munched her chocolate bar. 'Block up the roads with your four by fours, I should, you selfish lot!'

Mary hated being late for work. She considered it to be the height of bad manners. Thirty years, it had been thirty years since she'd begun driving along this route, since the day she'd got this job. She'd finally been given a job because she was good at it and not refused because of how she looked!

'Well, at least I didn't need to get a gastric band fitted!' she shouted to the four by four in front, as she resumed her musings. 'Now I can sit in my office and know I'm respected; respected because I'm bloody good at my job, and with luck, they've now learnt not to employ people based purely on how they look! Hopefully, they've realised those of us that are fat and plain work far harder because we don't get so many distractions from unwanted admirers! Most likely we'll never marry, and we're able to make the job a career and not just something to keep us in nail polish! We're able to come in early and to stay late because we don't have to rush off to pick up any little brats from school or rush home to prepare hubby a four-course dinner! I sometimes wonder if they realise how lucky they are to have us! Still, thank the lord; I'd finally been given a job that actually interested me, and I was able to stick two fingers up to all the doubters and say, 'Go to hell!' I went in there, and I showed them! I showed them the fat lady could work twice as hard as the pretty little stick insects that were forever running off to the restroom to powder their pretty little upturned noses … or taking time off to produce even more stick insects to infest the planet!' Mary now smiled smugly as she recalled the shock she'd got as she walked into the interview room, to find herself facing a beautiful, model like brunette displaying long shapely legs, elegantly crossed behind her keyhole desk!

'I'd never seen anyone quite so full of their own self-importance before!' she scoffed. 'She was so absorbed in presenting her own image she didn't care a toss how I looked!'

Then her eyes narrowed. 'It was a shame that trumped up little office girl in the typing pool found it so difficult to keep her thoughts to herself though. The little tart just couldn't resist whispering a bitchy remark to the girl sitting next to her, caring little if I heard or not. Did you really think I wouldn't hear it my dear, those words you whispered behind your red lacquered little fingernails?

'Look at the size of her!' she'd smirked, 'I bet she's only got the job so Boss Lady won't have any competition from her admirers!'

Oh yes, I heard you young lady! Just someone else who thought the fat woman didn't have any feelings! I didn't care though, I'd heard worse... and I'd got the job ... and now it's me doing the hiring... and the firing too–as you were very soon to find out my dear!

'OH, COME ON! I'm going to be late for the first time in thirty years if this damned traffic doesn't get a move on! Come on you stupid lot! What's the matter with you all this morning! For goodness sake pull your fingers out! It's only a bit of rain!'

Being late would soon be the last thing Mary would be worrying about; she'd find herself on a far more important journey than this—a journey that was to change her life completely.

Frank
Chapter 5

Frank sprung up athletically from his bedroom floor. 'Thirty press ups to start the day, there's nothing like it to get the adrenalin going and the blood coursing around the old body!'

He looked admiringly at his reflection in the full-length mirror on his wardrobe door, as he flexed his ample muscles. Pleased with what he saw, he smiled as his bronzed, taut and trim figure gleamed back at him. Frank was not a tall man, just five feet six inches, but he'd always worked out, and what he lacked in height he'd made up for in muscle. He was extremely proud of his toned and sturdy frame. He pulled on a pair of black jogging trousers before grabbing a matching top from his colour coordinated and extremely tidy wardrobe. He then admired himself once more in the mirror before walking jauntily into the kitchen of his first floor flat and heading for the fridge.

'Right, now for some breakfast!' he muttered, before opening the fridge door and peering at the neatly stocked shelves inside. 'Good morning Fridge,' he announced brightly, 'and what delights have you in store for me this morning?' An array of healthy options met his eye; fresh fruit and vegetables, fish and eggs—nothing

23

with added sugar and certainly no processed food! 'Mm,' he ruminated, 'carrot juice or cabbage detox? I think I'll do the detox today if I may Fridge—I did carrots yesterday.'

He took out a jug of ghastly green slimy looking liquid in front of him and poured some into a glass. He took a sip and savoured the feeling of thick glutinous fluid sliding down his throat.

'Mm, that is delicious! I can even feel it doing me good! Now a couple of miles around the block before I head to work, and I'll be ready to start my day! I'd better get my lunch packed up first though; they'll only be serving rubbish in the café again I suppose. The things people eat that they think are healthy for them, is beyond me! Ah, well, it keeps me in work I suppose.' He examined his fridge once more. 'Right Fridge, I'll do a low calorie, high protein lunch today I think.'

He carefully measured a cup of three bean salad and three ounces of chicken which he put into a plastic container, before draining the rest of his drink. 'I must remember to make some more high fibre drinks when I get home tonight too,' he informed the fridge as he rinsed his glass, before putting it neatly into the dishwasher.

Frank didn't like silence, but he liked the sound of a radio blaring out in the morning even less. A radio, he thought, brought either bad news or loud pop music hammering away inside your head; neither he felt being a suitable or healthy way for him to begin his day. So Frank talked. He talked to anything and everything, the walls, the doors, the fridge, the washing machine, anything that would listen to him without answering him back. He did at one time contemplate getting a cat but soon decided against it when he thought of all the disgusting, unhealthy animal hairs that would get into his food and cling onto his clothes and furniture. That, he decided, would cause him more anxiety than a blaring radio, and so Frank talked—to himself.

He walked into his pristine living room and plumped up an already plumped cushion. He looked out of the rain-streaked window.

'I think I'll hit the gym at lunchtime as the weather looks so grim. I could do with a weights work out anyway—mustn't forget the old pecs! Now Calendar, what do you have in store for me today?'

He headed across the room towards the small calendar standing erect on the highly polished sideboard.

'Ah, yes, squash night! Dave will be trying to beat me in the league tables! I'd better watch out for him! It's a good job I chose the cabbage detox for breakfast; I'll need the increased brain power to keep myself focussed for that! Keep on your toes, Frank; pace, pace, pace, that's the answer! Don't let the young whipper-snapper get the better of you! I hope he's prepared for me to run him off his feet! He won't know what's hit him! I certainly won't tire before he does, no matter what the age difference! Now, where are my wet weather running shoes?'

He went back into his bedroom and opened a cupboard which contained a full shoe rack of various styles of trainers, all designed to do a different job. He eventually chose a pair of *Nike* wet weather running shoes for jogging to work and a pair of blue *Salming* squash shoes, to give himself every advantage in his match against Dave later on in the day. He knew the rest of the equipment he needed would be at the gym and so he closed the cupboard door, put his lunch-box and his squash shoes into his sports bag, put on his wet weather trainers and headed for the front door.

Frank was now fifty and past his prime, but he was determined to keep himself as fit as he possibly could, regularly buying the latest keep-fit magazines to inspire him. He was well aware he was no longer as fast as he used to be around the squash court but he also knew if he used his brain he was still capable of holding his own against the younger players, after all it was only a game like snooker really, a game that just required you to leave your opponent in a difficult position! He knew if he was clever he could run the younger player around the court, wearing him down, thereby saving his own precious energy. He prided himself he was still able to take on and beat, young men less than half his age. He always found great pleasure after the match telling them they needed to 'up their energy levels' if they wanted to beat him! He knew in his heart his winning days were numbered, but, if he kept up his fitness regime, he thought he had a good ten years left in him yet. Sport had always been Frank's life and he dreaded the day when he'd no longer be able to partake in it. At least his job meant he had the facilities to be able to keep up his strict training schedule without it bankrupting him.

He worked as a personal trainer in a gym linked to the NHS. A new scheme had not long been introduced, offering obese patients referrals by their GPs if they were thought to be at risk of developing type 2 Diabetes, or if they needed to gain strength in their limbs after an accident or illness. By encouraging a new lifestyle, and changing eating habits, alongside an exercise programme, the government thought they could indirectly save money for the NHS. Frank took his work very seriously and had become very good at it. Motivation was a key area and he gained great fulfilment when he saw his methods were achieving positive results.

Unperturbed by the inclement weather Frank did his two-mile run around the block before heading to the gym, and as he ran, he planned the strategies he would use for beating Dave on the squash court later that day.

Little did he know he would soon have more than a game of squash to plan his strategies for, or that he'd be taking on an opponent who would be more of a challenge than he could ever have imagined.

Brendon
Chapter 6

'Thanks for driving me to school Dad.'

'I'm glad you appreciate how lucky you are, on such a miserable morning, Lucinda!' replied her father. 'I'm hoping I might also get a chance to intercept Mark Jonson as he drops Dillon off to school as well. I want to tell him I shall require his help giving out the hymn books in church on Sunday. I need an extra pair of hands, so I can support Reverend Graham. He will need me to be his right hand man and stand next to him as he welcomes the parishioners into church when they arrive.'

Even though it was raining heavily, Brendon was feeling good this morning. He was feeling good because yesterday the vicar told him he didn't know what he would do without him—and Brendon needed to feel appreciated, needed to feel valued! His mind veered away from his daughter sitting in the passenger seat beside him, as, with a smug smile, he began to contemplate all his 'good deeds'. He was a reliable and respected member of the school PTA, a stalwart of the church, and of course, there was the golf club—not that he played much golf but joining had meant he'd met a great many influential people in the clubhouse! He also prided himself on being a perfect host at the many dinner parties he'd held in his home.

'I hardly have any time left to myself these days, Lucinda,' he told his daughter. 'It becomes very tiring having to think about others and to organise them the way I do. I doubt things would run so smoothly if it weren't for me! Your mother's constantly nagging me, telling me I shouldn't be quite so generous with my time, but I tell her, if you expect people to look up to you in life, then you have to work at it!'

He paused to give a self-satisfied grin. Then Lucinda noticed his expression change as his eyes narrowed and his smile turned into a frown. She noticed the tone of his voice change as he continued.

'The trouble is not everyone is like me Lucinda. People will do anything to get out of doing a bit of extra work. The only way to get things done in this life is to ask folk straight out, military style, particularly with the menial tasks, otherwise I'd be left to do them all myself! I like to think of myself as their 'front man', their 'commanding officer'. There are others far more suited to the menial tasks than am I!' He nodded as if to confirm this thought to himself before continuing. 'Every Sunday I give up my time to pass out hymn books and never miss a week! I always have a word of welcome for each of the parishioners, and they like that! I need to be 'on the door'! The Vicar needs a respectable, trusted pillar of society for that. Things like pouring out coffee can be left to those not gifted with the same 'front of house' experience.'

'Yes Dad.' Although Lucinda had heard these words many times before, she also knew her father would expect to hear her agreeing with his words of wisdom. The last thing she wanted to do was to antagonise him this morning. She shot a surreptitious look across at him and could see by the set of his jaw she needed to be careful today not to make him angry.

However, Brendon was now busy thinking about the dinner party he'd held the previous Saturday evening. 'It's such a shame everyone had to go home so early, but I suppose the vicar was right to remind us we all had to be up early for church the next day.' He smiled smugly as he recalled Reverend Graham telling him how much he'd enjoyed the evening before he left!

'I must try to catch your Head Master and see if he enjoyed the evening too Lucinda. Perhaps I'll ring him later. I expect he'll be busy with the new intake this morning.'

Brendon shook his head and frowned. 'I can't think why he declined my offer of help. I'm sure an extra pair of hands would have been useful to him while he was getting everyone settled in.'

Lucinda's mind had drifted away from her father and was now thinking of Danny and the text he'd sent her, but she was brought quickly back to reality as her father shouted. 'It's best to get to know these people

Lucinda. You never know when they can be of use to you! You need to learn from that my girl! I joined the golf club even though I didn't play, and it's been a great way of meeting people. There's always such a mix of influential and professional people in the clubhouse, PLO's I call them: People like ourselves!' He laughed smugly at his little joke, before continuing with more wise words that Lucinda had heard not for the first time.

'You'll thank me one day my girl, later in your life, when you realise just how much I've sacrificed in order to pay for your private education! Money I've had to scrimp and save, to allow you to mix with the right sort of people!'

Lucinda had to turn her head away and look out of the side window, so her father wouldn't see her raise her eyes to the heavens. She'd heard this so many times before!

He slowed down and pulled into the side of the road outside the school, stopping on the hatched 'No Parking' area which ran along its entire length.

'Here we are Lucinda; I'm not going all the way down the drive this morning, you can get out here. Quickly now! Dillon's father's just going past! He must be dropping Dillon off further up the road! Hurry up! I need to catch up with him before he drives off! Come on, hurry up girl, it won't hurt you to run up the drive! And straight in! I don't want to see you stopping and talking to anyone!'

'No Dad. I won't. Bye.' She grabbed her school bag and then leant over to give her dad a peck on his cheek.

'I haven't got time for that nonsense Lucinda! Quickly, out now or I'll miss Mark Jonson!'

Lucinda had learnt from experience not to cross her father when he used that tone of voice and so she quickly leapt out of the little red Volkswagen Polo and, avoiding the puddles, began to run towards the school entrance, hesitating briefly by one of the pillars to pull out a red umbrella from her school bag.

Brendon, his mind focused on intercepting Mark, pulled out into the fast moving traffic. Unfortunately, he was so distracted watching where Mark was going to park his car and determined to ambush him before he drove off again, that he forgot to check in his rear view mirror before pulling out. The silver four x four coming up at full speed behind him had to brake violently in order to miss him, causing the big car to swerve, sending it skidding on the wet surface of the road.

Mary pleased that the traffic was at last flowing, was following closely behind the 4x4 and had to stamp on her brakes to try to avoid ramming into it. But standing water meant her tyres couldn't get a grip on the surface of the road and her Ford Fiesta slid helplessly, slamming into the back of it, sending the larger vehicle careering across to the other side of the busy main road. Unable to gain control of her car Mary mounted the pavement and could only look in horror as she saw the enormous pillars that adorned the school entrance coming towards her—and even worse the look of terror in the eyes of a girl with a red umbrella who was trapped in her pathway, as she ploughed head on into the car coming out of the school drive!

The bus driver coming in the opposite direction had no time to brake or to take any evasive action. The passengers on the bus looked in horror when they heard him curse loudly before ploughing into the side of the 4x4. They were then thrown viciously forward as they felt the impact. The bus ricocheted as it bounced off the wagon, and then careered across the road, hitting a telegraph pole. It then spun round 90 degrees and, as if in slow motion, gracefully overturned. Then everything went deathly quiet!

Brendon, totally oblivious to the chaos he had caused behind him, drove eagerly on to waylay the poor unsuspecting Mark. Then came a piercing scream!

Danny
Chapter 7

Danny walked along the street with the rhythm of Tinie Tempah blasting from his headphones. The lyrics always seemed to mean something to him. As he took in the words of 'Turn the Music Louder' he strode out in time to the beat, oblivious of the rain, of his sodden trainers or of the busy morning traffic. He looked up just in time to avoid walking into a lamppost and as he looked the short distance ahead, he saw the lovely Lucinda Green getting out of her father's car. His heart missed a beat as he dug his mobile phone out of his pocket once more to see if she had returned his text. No, still no reply! If only girls would realise how difficult boys found it to ask them out they wouldn't be quite so heartless! How stupid he felt. How was he ever going to look her in the eye again? He imagined the smirks and giggles he would get from the other girls and the ribbing he would have to endure from the boys.

'It'll be all round the school by the time that I get there,' he told himself. 'How am I ever going to face her? If only I'd thought before I pressed that send button!'

He slowed his steps, not wanting to catch up with her, and hung back as he watched her get out her red umbrella. She even looked good with rain soaked hair!

He raised his phone in order to take a surreptitious video and through his viewfinder he saw her turn to wave a half-hearted goodbye to her father, before turning back towards the school gates. He watched as her father pulled out into the traffic. He saw the 4x4 coming up at speed having to brake. He froze as the car behind it went into a skid and, as if paralysed, he stood open mouthed as Lucinda was flung high into the air. All he could think was that she looked like Mary Poppins holding on to her red umbrella—while all the time the rhythm of Tinie Tempah pounded in his ears. He stood there, wide-eyed and quite still, unable to move, until a scream suddenly brought him back to his senses and propelled him forward. He knew he must get to her. He must help her!

He was the first person to reach her and there was so much blood! He knelt beside her and took off his anorak to cover her and keep her warm and dry. Her dazed and puzzled eyes looked up at him, confused.

'You didn't reply to my text,' was all he could think of saying. He was annoyed with himself for saying such a stupid, pathetic thing!

'What happened?' she whispered weakly, ignoring his words.

'A car skidded on the wet road—don't worry you're going to be fine.'

'Dad?' she questioned.

Danny looked up, wildly searching the faces of those now gathered about him.

'Has anyone phoned for an ambulance?' he shouted.

'Yes, I have, they'll be here soon,' came a distant voice from somewhere behind him.

His eyes scanned the scene in front of him, and all he could see was chaos! Pedestrians were trying their best to help the injured passengers in the two crumpled cars blocking the school's entrance gates. In the middle of the main road people were crowded around a crushed 4x4—and further across the road he could see a bus, which was lying on its side. Danny had never felt so frightened. He looked down at Lucinda, her eyes kept closing as if she just wanted to sleep.

'Don't go to sleep Luce. Stay awake till the ambulance gets here.'

He didn't really know why he told her that, although he thought he may have heard someone say it in a movie.

'Will you stay with me Dan, come in the ambulance with me?' she pleaded, unable to hide her fear.

'Course I will Luce, don't worry, I'm not going to leave you for a minute.'

It seemed like an eternity to him before the ambulances finally arrived. During that time, he'd held Lucinda's hand and watched her drift in and out of consciousness. Once they arrived he was relieved when the ambulance crew took over.

'Can I come in the ambulance with her?' he asked.

'Yes lad. Get in.'

Once at the hospital, Lucinda was quickly taken into an examination room and he was left alone, feeling uncomfortable, out of place and frightened, not really knowing what he should do next. He was looking down at his wet, blood-stained school shirt when a policewoman came up to him.

'My, you're a wet one aren't you? Are you OK love? You better get out of those wet clothes! Did you see the accident? Can you tell me what happened?'

Thinking quickly and not wanting to get Lucinda's father into trouble, Danny told the policewoman all he'd seen was the 4x4 going into a skid on the wet road. He immediately felt guilty about lying and not telling her he'd witnessed Lucinda's father pulling out into the traffic without looking. He knew in his heart what he was doing was wrong. He'd been brought up to always tell the truth. Although he hadn't really told a lie—had he? He'd just not told her everything! He could visualise how disappointed his dad would be if he became aware of what he'd done. But he was only trying to protect Lucinda! She'd be devastated if she found out it was her father who'd been responsible for the pain she was suffering; that just wouldn't be fair. Surely, she'd got enough to cope with right now. He couldn't be that cruel to her, could he?

Then he saw her father!

Brendon Green, wearing a camel coloured Crombie coat with a brown velvet collar and highly polished brown shoes, strode briskly across the ward. It wasn't a new coat; he'd bought it on e-bay at a good price. However, it made him feel good, it made him feel 'someone'! He clutched his brown trilby hat against his puffed-out chest as he crossed over to speak to the nurse on duty. His neatly trimmed moustache appeared to be twitching with rage!

Brendon had never been in the army but dressing as he thought a sergeant major would dress gave him a feeling of authority. He wanted the world to see him as a figure of power that should be looked up to—not an insignificant nobody to be cast aside! All his life he'd been made to feel like nothing. When young he'd been in and out of care homes, the little urchin boy from a bad home—well not anymore! Now he intended to show them! Now he not only looked respectable, he was also a respected member of society. People spoke of him as 'that dapper little man, always full of his own self-importance', and they were right, because for Brendon image was vitally important. It was the way he could show everyone how influential he was and how he had no intention of being messed around!

'I wish to see my daughter, Lucinda Green.' His booming voice echoed across the waiting area. 'Take me to her please!'

Surprised by the unfriendly attitude coming from the man in front of her and annoyed by his tone, the pretty young nurse looked up from the computer in front of her.

'Good morning Sir. I believe Lucinda's in the examination room now being assessed. The waiting room is just along the corridor. If you'd like to go there, I'll come and fetch you as soon as the doctor has dealt with her.'

'Perhaps you didn't hear me young lady. I wish to see her NOW! I also want to speak to the doctor and not to his minion. Show me where he is at once! If you don't I warn you I will be speaking to my MP. I have friends in very high places you know!'

'Could I have a word with you first sir?' asked the policewoman, who had seen a tricky situation about to develop and was doing her best to intercept before it got out of hand.

Brendon turned slowly around to face the policewoman, his eyes narrowing, his anger beginning to boil just below the surface.

'No officer, you cannot!' he snarled between clenched teeth. 'My daughter was caught up in all this mayhem this morning, and I have no intention of speaking to anyone until I have spoken to her. I know my rights and I do not expect to be fobbed off. I wish to see her, and I wish to see her right now. I have no intention of taking no for an answer!'

The officer picked up Brendon's mode of speech and returned in the same pace and tone.

'I'm sure you'll be allowed to see her as soon as her injuries have been assessed sir. You must understand the doctors are very busy now trying to help all those that were injured. Were you at the scene sir? Have you any idea what caused the accident?'

'I am not concerned with any of the others that have been injured officer! My only concern is with my daughter! As for what caused the accident, I would have thought that was obvious, people driving like lunatics on wet roads of course! I myself had driven away only moments earlier; otherwise I could be lying in one of those hospital beds too! Something needs to be done! Someone needs to be punished for this! Perhaps if there had been more police presence to slow the traffic the whole thing may well have been avoided!'

'This young man kindly accompanied your daughter in the ambulance Sir,' informed the policewoman, trying to avoid any further confrontation by changing the subject, thereby hoping to defuse the irate man's rant. Brendon turned his glare towards Danny, his eyes taking in his blood-stained shirt and his expression changed in a moment from one of anger to one of pure hate.

'Did he indeed? Well he had no right! I'll ask you not to interfere with something that doesn't concern you! So you can be on your way young man!'

Danny stepped back, his eyes wide, his mouth dropped open in surprise. He couldn't believe his ears! How could the man be so arrogant! Surely this wasn't

Lucinda's father, she was always so softly spoken and so kind. Perhaps if he realised he was the one responsible for all the chaos going on about them he would change his tune! To think he had tried to protect this man. However, dobbing him in now wasn't going to help Lucinda. He must wait until the time was right!

Alan
Chapter 8

It had started like any other miserable Monday morning. Alan walked half a mile to the bus stop, his head down as the rain lashed into him, feeling like small pebbles being flung into his face. Both his beige raincoat, with its collar turned up, and his scarf, which was tucked into his neck, were already soaked through. His umbrella had blown inside out twice in the strong, gale force wind, making his once neatly parted hair stand on end. Although he'd tried to walk as far away from the gutter as he possibly could, the spiteful drivers, full of their own importance and having no thought for mere pedestrians, had purposely driven their cars through the puddles, splashing him and his black leather briefcase and leaving the bottoms of his pin-striped trousers wet and soggy. They now clung wretchedly to his ankles, making him feel even more miserable and irritable than usual.

He cursed inwardly as the 8.05 bus was late yet again and the long queue made it impossible to wait undercover in the bus shelter, causing more annoyance as he became wetter still! When the wretched thing eventually arrived, fifteen minutes later, it was full, adding to the unpleasantness as he had to stand; feeling hemmed in and squashed by the soggy, stale smelling people clustered about him. Infuriated he couldn't shut them out as he usually did by looking out of the window or doing the Telegraph crossword, he inwardly seethed, hanging on to the overhead strap and glaring whenever someone lost their balance and dared to invade his space.

Alan, a very quiet, deep thinking person, was unmarried and lived alone. He was an avid games player and an enjoyable evening for him was playing Bridge online with other serious, like-minded people, people with whom he had little or no contact or interest, except at the online Bridge table. He took everything in life seriously and rarely laughed. He found making conversation difficult and when forced at work to do so, he would keep his eyes fixed firmly on his paper-work, never looking his opposite number in the eye. When interaction with his fellow man became unavoidable, he would extricate himself from the predicament as quickly as he possibly could.

Alan worked in the accounts department at Morgan and Taylor, a large department store in the centre of town. He was good at his job and found the situation ideal as no one had cause to venture into his office very often. He always preferred to keep himself to himself and was most content when at home, with his nose inside a good book or with his headphones on and his eyes closed, as he imagined conducting one of his favourite Beethoven symphonies.

Today however, he felt incensed by having to make bodily contact with people he neither knew nor indeed ever wanted to know, as the bus bumped and swerved its way along Wellington Street. He was infuriated by all the chatter going on about him. Why couldn't people just go quietly on their journey? Why did they feel the need to share how much they disliked the bad weather? We all dislike bad weather but some of us don't feel the need to discuss it! He felt tense and cross. Just another dreary, dismal day like any other!

THEN: suddenly he was flying through the air! People and their luggage began being tossed about, crashing in all directions, banging into one another and screaming—screaming!

'What the hell?'

Bodies were being flung everywhere, falling on top of him—and people were shouting and moaning!

Then silence! Darkness!

When he came to it was so quiet except for an occasional groaning sound. Someone uttered a cry, or had that been him? Was that weird sound really coming from his mouth?

Oh how his foot hurt!

He was lying on the floor, his head pressed hard up against the back of a seat. He felt confused. He tried to take things in, to make sense of what had happened.

'If only I could free my foot,' he thought. 'I can't move my foot. It must be stuck, trapped under something!'

He looked up and made out the shape of a young girl wearing a blue school uniform. She couldn't be more than thirteen years old, and she was lying on the floor a little way from him, her once blonde hair now streaked with blood—so much blood!

'Please help me!' she whispered, her innocent blue eyes looking into his.

He could hear people all about him groaning, but because of the angle he was lying at he was unable to see them.

'I should help them! I think I should help them!'

But what could he do, he couldn't move! A voice raged inside his head.

'Free your foot! Get your head together man!' He then remembered the schoolboy first aid he'd learnt all those years before, when his mother, much against his will, had insisted he should go to Scouts.

'I need to help the girl! I must help the girl first! She needs me to help her!'

Even though his foot was still stuck it wasn't hurting quite as much as it had initially and slowly he managed to slither his body the few inches needed to be nearer to her. Although still disoriented he was aware the gash on her head needed covering!

'Damn this foot! I can't move it! … Come on man, think! My scarf use that! Cover her head wound with that! Use it as a bandage! THINK MAN!'

It seemed to take forever but somehow, in his confused state, he managed to wriggle out of his raincoat, which seemed to be trapped underneath him, allowing the movement necessary to get a little closer to the girl. He then unwound the scarf about his neck.

'This should do the job', he thought, or did he say it out loud, he wasn't sure. He tried to wrap the scarf around her head but couldn't get near enough to her and so she had to help him by holding it in position. They tried, between them, to tie the scarf in place and, after a considerable amount of determination, and for what seemed like an age, he finally secured it as best he could. It was crude, and he knew he'd never win a prize for nurse of the year, but it was the best he could do in the circumstances.

'At least,' he thought, 'it'll keep her wound clean for now.'

The child seemed to relax a little after that and Alan shouted to her.

'Come on girl; don't go to sleep on me now, not now I've tried to help you!'

He was rewarded with the most beautiful smile, a smile he would always remember.

'NO! Don't go to sleep on me child! You mustn't go to sleep! Sing! Let's sing! What do we both know?

THE WHEELS ON THE BUS GO ROUND AND ROUND ….
Come ON, sing with me! I'm not going to sing alone!
Good! Now keep singing while I look after that lady
there! THE WHEELS ON THE BUS GO ROUND AND
ROUND…'

The grey-haired lady to his right was bleeding
heavily from her leg. He wriggled across to her. She
looked so pale and fragile—and very frightened.

'My tie—I can use that—make a tourniquet—
where is everyone? COME ON, WE NEED HELP IN HERE!
Come on girl, keep singing! THE WHEELS ON THE BUS…

They were trapped like that for what seemed to
Alan, like hours, and during that time he led the singing,
until the fire brigade were finally able to cut them free.

'How are they?' one of the firemen asked a
doctor.

'The girl will be fine I think, just a few stitches and
maybe a bit of concussion, and thankfully the old lady's
bleeding has been stemmed by the tourniquet, but the
man's in a bad way I'm afraid, looks like he could lose his
leg!'

Tess
Chapter 9

Tess always took her work very seriously; she didn't know how to do it any other way. She knew, as far as the school was concerned, her subject was way down at the bottom of the pile. However, she didn't see it that way, for her it was vitally important. It was her job to guide her pupils to help them build their self-esteem. Other subjects built intelligence, but her subject helped them gain confidence, the confidence they would need to achieve their goals. She felt responsible for each and every pupil put into her care. She felt responsible for any thoughts, ideas or information she put before them. Each 'child' was important to her. Each child became her responsibility.

As she looked at her new class (each wearing a pristine navy-blue blazer that was yet to see a muddy playground or patched elbow), she noted their expectant faces, fresh, nervous and excited, as they looked up at her. She felt her stomach somersault and her spirits rise. She realised she had an important duty to fulfil and she felt her life had purpose once again.

One child in particular intrigued her. She sat alone, shoulders tense and arms clasped about her. Her head was down, her eyes up, but focused only on Tess, as if distancing herself from all the other pupils. Her eyes were questioning, summing up, working out if Tess could be trusted. This child was not going to offer herself easily. Tess knew it would take time to gain her trust and realised she needed to take care. She knew there were deep feelings inside that tense little body, if only she would relax enough to release them. She reminded Tess of herself; someone who would never quite feel she belonged, that she would never fit in, hiding her true self from the world. Tess remembered how set apart she'd always felt when she lived at home with her parents and how she never had anything in common with her perfect sister, the perfect sister that was idolised by her mother because, unlike her, she never did anything wrong!

She was halfway through her welcoming lesson, designed to bond the class on their first morning when she heard the door keypad clicking, followed by a knock on her door.

'Could I have a quick word with you Ms Matthews?' asked the voice of the school secretary, as her head peered around the door.

Puzzled, Tess slipped outside the classroom, to see what was so important as to make someone from above come down to see her in her dungeon.

'I'm so sorry to disturb your class Ms Matthews, but there's been a most terrible accident outside the school gates, involving both parents and pupils I'm afraid. Sadly, the mother of one of your class was involved. Her car was hit head-on as she was waiting at the gate to exit the grounds and sadly she died at the scene.' Tess went cold as past memories crowded in on her. 'I'm afraid I'm going to have to take the child out of your lesson, so that the Head can inform her.'

Somehow, some sixth sense perhaps, Tess knew exactly which child it was going to be before she was told. She knew it would be the child with the distant eyes, and a deep feeling of empathy encased her as she remembered her own loss. She had known what it was like to lose someone at the centre of her world. When it had happened to her she had been an adult and yet she had totally fallen apart, unable to confide in anyone. So how was this young child going to come to terms with such a loss?

Tess also knew she mustn't let her feelings get the better of her because she still had to go back inside the classroom and continue teaching the other twenty-six children waiting for her magic.

A confused Daisy was taken up to the Head's office, where worried faces greeted her to tell her the devastating news. There's no easy way to tell a child such a life-changing story. Daisy didn't cry as they had expected, she just stared back at them with steely eyes, daring them not to comfort her. She nodded as she took in their words, as if something she'd been expecting had finally been confirmed.

'Someone will take you to your grandmothers Daisy. She is expecting you.'

'Could the lady that was teaching me take me please?' Daisy spoke hesitantly, not totally understanding why she was making this request but conscious of the fact it was the right thing for her to do.

Surprised, Mr Hinton, Linford School's Head Master, looked over his half-rimmed spectacles and enquired gently, 'Ms Matthews? Well, she has a class to teach my dear, but I'm sure something can be arranged, just wait here a while Daisy and I'll see what I can do.' He rose from behind the enormous oak desk that stood grandly in front of the large sash window, which looked out onto the sports field. Then, with some relief, he left the room, leaving Daisy with the school secretary and another lady she had never seen before.

Daisy sat with her hands in her lap waiting. It was very quiet in there. She noticed a picture on the wall of an old man looking very grim, standing at the top of the steps in front of the school's entrance doors. She looked at the caption underneath the picture which said, 'Sir William Linford'. She noticed the many photographs on the wall around him, of pupils holding trophies, or sitting in their sports clothes holding tennis racquets, hockey sticks or rugger balls and she wondered if they'd ever sat in the chair that she sat in now. She listened as the second hand of the clock on the wall ticked by. No one spoke to her. No one seemed to know what to say and tension hung in the air. Much to her relief, the door finally opened, and Tess walked in. Daisy got up from her chair without a word and walked across the room to her, taking the hand that Tess held out in front of her.

51

They drove in silence as Tess took Daisy to her grandmother's home and the only form of contact they had was when she felt the child's small hand slip into hers, as they walked up the drive towards the front door.

A distraught, elderly, white-haired lady was standing on the front porch of a warden-controlled bungalow, who Tess presumed to be Daisy's grandmother. She was being comforted by another lady of about the same age. As Daisy and Tess drew near, she hugged Daisy's grandmother before waddling off towards an identical bungalow next door. The grandmother held open her arms and Daisy walked into them. She then wrapped them around the child and sobbed as she rocked Daisy back and forth. After a while Daisy pulled away, uncomfortable with her grandmother's show of emotion. She looked up at Tess, who could see that her pupil's remote eyes were still totally dry.

Inside the bungalow, Tess was offered a cup of tea which she accepted. She knew that anything would be better for the old lady than to sit down, she needed something to do! She was also aware anything would be better for the child at that moment than to experience her grandmother's grief. They sat side by side on the worn, beige settee, with its hand crocheted antimacassar and arm caps—pupil and teacher. Both knowing, yet both puzzled how much they understood and needed each other at that time.

'It's just the two of us now Daisy,' sniffed her grandmother pathetically when she brought the tea-cosy clad teapot back into the living room. They watched in silence as the old lady poured the tea through a strainer, listening to it splash into the cups. Then, with shaking hands, she passed Tess a gold-rimmed china cup and saucer, decorated with red roses. 'We need to look after each other now, don't we love?' Once again Daisy's sad eyes burned into Tess's soul, and Tess gently reached across and laid her free hand over Daisy's. She then spoke very softly to her.

'It's too soon to try and take it all in my love or to make sense of it. Let the next few days, weeks, take what they need from you. It will end eventually, and all will become clear. Don't try to fathom it out now.' Daisy managed the slightest of nods, as if she already knew the outcome.

Tess stayed with the little girl and her grandmother for a short while. Before she left the bungalow, she handed the child a piece of paper on which she'd written her address and telephone number.

'I'm here for you Daisy. Call me at any time. I'm here for you if you need me.' Again, that slight nod said it all and Tess got up and let herself out of the bungalow. When she'd got into her car and begun the drive back to the school, unable to hold back the tears streaming down her cheeks, she suddenly realised that from the time she'd first seen Daisy in the classroom until now, she'd never heard the child speak. So much had passed between them and yet Daisy had never uttered a single word.

So, began a relationship that was to develop over the next few years. Here began a new beginning for both of them, a time to lose themselves and to find themselves again—although it would be a while before either of them realised this.

Nurse Joyce Jones
Chapter 10

'Mum, where are my trainers?'

'I don't know. Where did you take them off?'

'I can't remember.'

It happened every morning, but still, Joyce Jones ran up the stairs to help her son find his missing footwear.

'What's for breakfast?' This came from Son Number Two, who she bumped into as he was on his way to the bathroom. Well, at least he was intending to wash today so that was a plus.

'Get whatever you want. I haven't got time to cook this morning. Get some cereal.'

You know I hate cereal.'

'Well some toast then!'

'I thought you said breakfast was the most important meal of the day.'

'Well, I'm pleased at least some of my words of wisdom managed to hit home. If you'd wanted a cooked breakfast you should have got up at the same time as your Dad.'

By now Son Two had disappeared into the bathroom, slamming the door behind him and Joyce took a deep breath as she ventured into the bedroom of Son Number One, to hopefully find the missing trainers.

Joyce should have been used to this morning banter, as it, or something similar, happened most mornings and yet her boys could still manage to wind her up. It always ended in a rush for her to get out of the door and to work on time.

Her husband was first to go out each morning and once she'd made his breakfast, put his sandwiches in his hand and waved him off, it was time to get the boys out of bed—which was never easy, as being on time for college was not high on their list of priorities.

Joyce was able to run her ward in the hospital like clockwork but getting three men up for work was a different kettle of fish.

'Will up two hurry up? If you want a lift to college you'd better be downstairs in five minutes or you'll have to walk—and it's raining!' she shouted as she ran downstairs. 'I'm not going to be late again!'

Joyce was never actually late but she didn't intend to tell her son's that.

By the time she arrived at the hospital she was exhausted. She had only been there for about twenty minutes before being told patients from an RTC were due in. She was busy enough without that. Where was she going to put them all? The A&E department usually ran smoothly but on mornings like this she didn't know which way to turn. Everyone seemed to be asking her questions at the same time! She looked about her. Not only could she see patients needing her help, but the ward was also buzzing with police officers and worried looking visitors, all anxious to speak to her!

Well patients first!

'Right everyone, listen up,' she announced in her most commanding voice, having gathered all her team around her in order to brief them. 'This is what we have in from the RTC.'

She referred to her list, while tucking a strand of mousy hair that had escaped from her cap back into its rightful place. She then began to reel off the list in front of her.

'We have a male, mid-forties, with a serious leg injury'. She looked up and cast her eyes over the little group of expectant faces in front of her. 'He is in surgery as we speak but it appears we may be looking at an amputation.'

She looked back to her list. 'We have a seventy-three-year-old woman in bed four, with leg lacerations... a thirteen-year-old girl in bed two with a head injury and possible concussion... a sixteen year old girl with a broken arm and possible internal injuries, she's being examined upstairs at the moment but should be coming down to us very shortly... we have a forty-eight year old woman, who it says here has multiple injuries. I'm not sure yet what those injuries are but I'll let you know as soon as I hear from above. At some point they'll be sending a twenty five year old woman to us with a possible spine injury. That's all I have for you at the moment. There were other casualties, but they were mostly children on their way to school and they've gone onto the children's ward, so if anyone comes asking for them send them down there.'

She hesitated as she read her notes. 'I see there was another lady, um… Ms Rebecca Miller, but she was taken straight down to the morgue I'm afraid.' Nurse Jones looked up once more and took in the sympathetic faces of her nursing staff. 'You need to know this in case we have any relations phoning in and asking for her whereabouts. In which case, I'm sure I have no need to tell you to please be sensitive and discreet, and should they come in person then take them into the relative's room, where I'll come and speak to them.'

Having absorbed her list of patients now came the time for Nurse Jones to delegate jobs to her team.

'The patients with multiple injuries are still being assessed at the moment, however, we'll need beds made up and ready for when they do come down to us. One at least—the possible amputation, will be going into Critical Care for a few days.'

She then smiled. 'Just another day at the office I'm afraid—looks like it could be a busy one!' Her years of experience had taught her she needed to put her nurses at ease. She had to show her staff that she was calm and unflappable if she was to gain their confidence and to set the mood for the day. The last thing she wanted was everyone running around like headless chickens!

'Nurse Palmer—Bed three, men's ward—his drip needs changing... and Nurse Pitman, will you go down to the Children's Ward please, to see if they have a bed for the thirteen-year-old girl? She'll be far better off down there with children of her own age. If that's not possible, then try to make sure the two younger RTC patients are in beds next door to each other.'

She then turned to speak to the young blonde nurse to her left. 'Nurse Williams, while Nurse Pitman is doing that, will you clean up the young girl in bed two? She only has superficial wounds I understand, but she looks a mess and she'll be frightened, so use your charm to try and put her at ease. I'm sure if you put your mind to it you'll be able to do that on the women's ward just as well as you do it on the men's!' A giggle went around the other nurses, caused more by relief of tension than anything else. 'The child's name is Alice Norton. She'll feel much better once she's had a clean head dressing. She may have concussion so keep an eye open for any sign of that too.'

Nurse Jones then continued with her instructions. 'We may have a problem when the older girl', she looked back to her notes, 'Lucinda Green, comes down onto the ward. You may well have heard her father causing some disturbance earlier! He is now in the relative's room but if he should cause any further problems please don't hesitate to get me at once. He must not be allowed onto the ward until we've had time to settle everyone in. We've enough to do without irate visitors!'

A general nod of agreement went round the nurses before Nurse Jones continued.

'The elderly lady in bed four, Margery Beddows, will need her leg dressing changed frequently, we don't want it to become ulcerated. Will you sort that Nurse Collins? She's a little anxious to call her daughter too, so perhaps you could deal with that as well?'

Nurse Jones hesitated to see if she had missed anything before continuing.

'Well I think that's about it! If there are any problems come and see me. Nurse Pitman, when you come back from the Children's Ward, could you see we have the beds made up for the three patients due to come down to us please; three on the women's ward and one on the men's. Sort the women's ward first as it seems likely they'll be the first ones down. Thank you everyone, if you have any problems come and find me!'

Pleased that everything was once again under at least some control, Nurse Joyce Jones gave a sigh of relief as she watched her team hurry off in all directions to carry out her orders. She then turned to go and attend to the paperwork, which was now piling up on her desk at the nurse's station. She walked across to the door, but before she went out her eyes flicked once more around her ward. She had a strong team of dedicated nurses and she knew all her patients were in very good hands. She hovered by bed four where Nurse Collins was already chatting to Margery Beddows, or rather Margery Beddows was chatting to Nurse Collins, who was listening attentively to whatever the old lady was telling her. The poor lady looked so worried and Nurse Joyce watched as the young auburn-haired nurse took her hand, before passing across the handbag lying at the end of the bed. Mrs Beddows fumbled in her bag for a while and then took out a notebook and pen and wrote something on a slip of paper, which she offered up to the nurse. Nurse Joyce smiled to herself as she heard the old lady say, 'She may be out shopping. I don't want to worry her, but my little dog will be all on her own and she'll need someone to go in and feed her! Milly always has her tea at five-o-clock and then she needs to be let outside for a wee.'

'Don't worry Mrs Beddows, I'll get in touch with your daughter immediately and let her know that you're in here and that Milly will need someone to look after her.'

'You won't worry my daughter, will you? She is so very busy with the children. Tell her I'm fine and I won't need her to come into the hospital to visit me; as long as she can organise somebody to look after Milly.'

'Now, don't you be worrying yourself Margery. Do you have any other children I need to call?'

'I have a son,' announced the old lady proudly, 'He's such a lovely boy! He works very hard. I think he may be abroad on business at the moment though—I haven't heard from him in a while—but I know he'll be in touch just as soon as he can! His wife needs him at weekends to ferry the children about to their various clubs. They're such very clever children! No, don't call him! I don't want to be a bother to them! When he does see me I'm sure he'll tell me off because I didn't have my mobile phone with me! I was in such a hurry to catch the bus that I left it on the kitchen table again!'

'Right, I'll phone your daughter now then, and if she's not in I'll be leaving a message for her to go and feed Milly. I'll ask her if she'll bring in your mobile phone when she comes, in case you need to get in touch with someone while you're in here.'

'I'm sure my neighbour wouldn't mind feeding Milly, she has a key, in case my daughter is busy!'

Nurse Collins laughed. 'Don't you worry yourself about Milly. I'll go and feed her myself if we can't get in touch with anyone!'

Nurse Joyce smiled. Yes, her staff could cope very well without her now and she turned her attention to the paperwork waiting for her at the Nurse's Station.

Valerie
Chapter 11

She lay, unmoving, staring up at a stain on the ceiling, her mind going over and over the last things she remembered before waking up in the hospital bed.

She was aware her mind hadn't been concentrating entirely on her driving, and she could recall the rain-soaked streets. She even remembered the car behind tooting when she hadn't noticed the traffic lights change to green—but that was all. She'd been told she'd been in an accident, but she couldn't remember it. All she could remember about that morning was that she needed to get home and put the 4x4 in the garage before her husband returned.

She could recall every tiny second of the previous evening though and was aware what she'd done was wrong. She knew perfectly well she shouldn't have met him. Her life had been happy enough before he'd come along. So why had she felt the need to turn it all on its head? Five idyllic years, she'd been content for five idyllic years, so why now? Why did she have to mess everything up now? There'd been no reason for her to be unfaithful. Ben was kind and loving and prosperous. He'd worked hard to make a good life for them. There wasn't even anything wrong with their sex life either, in fact, she had absolutely nothing to complain about. So why had she begun an affair with a man that meant nothing to her? Why was she so captivated by this man that she'd risked losing everything?

She'd spent the night in a hotel bedroom with someone, just because she'd found him exciting! Ben had been away on a business trip and she'd told him she was going up to London to spend the evening with some friends from her office! Instead she'd met Patrick. Patrick with his engaging Irish accent, Patrick with his amusing blarney! She knew she wasn't the first of his office dalliances, and she was also aware it wouldn't last or lead to anything—neither did she want it to—so why? Why take the risk of losing what she already had?

Her mind slipped back into the hotel bedroom as she replayed their evening together. It had been an evening consumed with, not love or logic, just a carnal act: a hunger that couldn't be satisfied until passions had been spent and tensions released. She knew there would be time for guilt later, but she was prepared to risk that for the wonderful feeling of being 'alive' again. This was a time for excitement, a time for shameless, uncontrolled passion.

The spot on the ceiling came back into focus. Now she felt dirty: no better than a prostitute! She wanted to turn over, to hide her head in her pillow but she wasn't even allowed that luxury. And she had brought it all upon herself, she who had always prided herself on having such high principles. She should have put a stop to it before it had got this far—but the fact was she was enjoying it! She was enjoying the excitement, the fun and the ADVENTURE! She was even aroused by the possibility that one day she may be found out! She'd become really good at lying to her husband and covering her tracks, it was all part of the game... And it was so stupid! Why the hell had she done it? Yet each time she decided to put an end to it, Patrick would be there offering her some new adventure. When she was with Patrick she felt good, she felt special, she felt alive— but afterwards, on the drive home, she always felt so ashamed, so disloyal, so tainted!

Ben had told her he'd wanted to start a family, and she'd led him to believe that she did too, and each day, when she secretly took her contraceptive pill, she did so with so much guilt! They'd been married for five years; she'd been just nineteen and he two years older. She was now twenty-four, a perfect time to become a parent, or so everyone thought. But not her, not yet! There'd be plenty of time for babies, but not yet. There was too much to see and too much to do for that! She wanted to see the world, to see life. Looking around at her friends proved when babies came along, seeing the world went out of the window.

So, she'd lied!

Her affair had been going on for six months and she was becoming used to her secret life. She was finding it increasingly easy to keep the two lives separate, in separate compartments, like Patrick had advised her.

She knew he was married, even knew his wife and was aware he had other women. She even knew Ben was twice the man Patrick would ever be—but Ben wasn't exciting! Ben had become predictable and boring!

So now here she lay in a hospital bed, with a brace around her neck... and as she lay there, unmoving, she wondered what she could possibly say to stop Ben finding out where she'd been, and how would he take the news she may never be able to carry his child?

Brendon
Chapter 12

Brendon was furious! How dare they treat him like this, it was HIS daughter for god sake, and he had rights! How dare they stick him in a waiting room as if he was no one!

Margaret Green pushed back the hood of her dark blue anorak as she entered the main doors of the hospital building and dripped her way across to the reception area. She looked worried and anxious as she scurried up to the enquiry desk.

'Um… er… excuse me Nurse. Could you tell me where my husband is, please? My daughter has been involved in a road accident. Her name is Lucinda Green,' she blurted out breathlessly.

She was a thin, sparrow-like, little woman, constantly looking about her as if she expected someone to jump out and attack her at any moment. Her handbag dangled from her arm and she held her hands clasped together in front of her as if begging.

The nurse behind the reception desk smiled. Yes, she knew very well where this timid lady's husband was. He was the one causing the disturbance in A&E earlier this morning. She'd already been briefed about him! She felt sorry for the mousey little woman who stood before her, who was obviously terrified of the dreadful man.

'Your husband's in the relative's waiting room Mrs Green. It's just down the corridor on the left. I understand your daughter is being assessed at the moment, but there'll be someone coming to take you to see her very soon.'

'Thank you very much,' whispered Maggie, now nervously playing with the straps of her handbag. 'Um ... do you know how my daughter is please?'

'No, not yet I'm afraid, but I promise that you'll be allowed to see her as soon as she's sent down onto the ward, Mrs Green. As we told your husband earlier, when we've got her settled in someone will come and collect you.'

'Yes, of course. Thank you. Thank you very much.' she whispered, before scurrying away down the corridor to find her husband.

Through the glass window of the door, Maggie could see Brendon was on his feet, pacing the floor and breathing heavily, as he slapped his thighs in irritation. His face was red and angry. She dreaded it when he was like this. With knuckles now white from clutching her handbag even tighter to her, she entered the waiting room. She already knew he would blame her, as he always did when things didn't quite go his way.

He swung around to face her.

'Where the hell have you been woman?' were the first thunderous words that came from his mouth, as he glared at her.

'I came as quickly as I could Brendon, but the traffic was dreadful this morning,' she babbled. 'The awful weather had caused a tailback, and the bus took ages to get through. They were very kind to me at work though and allowed me to leave as soon as you had spoken to them.'

'So I should think!'

Maggie Green didn't drive. Her husband wouldn't allow it. He said there was no point in her learning as it was his duty as a husband to do all the driving, but she sometimes wondered if this was just another of the methods he used to manipulate her. Each day he wanted to know exactly where she'd been and what she had been doing, who she'd spoken to and what had been said. He told her she was lucky to have such a devoted husband, that took so much interest in her menial affairs—and she believed him! He had kindly allowed both Lucinda and herself to have a mobile phone, but he'd programmed them, so he'd always know exactly where they were at every given moment of the day. He said it was for their safety and security, but Maggie had a suspicion it was really because he wanted to keep tabs on them.

'Have you found out what happened, Brendon? How is Lucinda?' her timorous voice dared to ask.

'How do you expect me to know what's going on woman when I'm locked away in here!' he snapped. 'I got a phone call on my way to work to tell me she'd been in an accident! I was on my way to discuss mortgages with a potential new customer—most inconvenient! I doubt I'll get that contract now!' He continued his pacing.

'I dropped her off right outside the school gates! Right outside! She should have gone straight inside, instead of hanging about the entrance for some young boy, like a street tart! He was here at the hospital when I arrived—how do you like that! They said he'd come in the ambulance with her! What right had he? How dare they take things into their own hands before speaking to me first? I sent him packing though! I thought I'd brought her up decently and how does she repay me? No better than a prostitute!' His threatening eyes swung around to Maggie and he came towards her, shouting into her face. 'I blame you—always giving in to her! Always allowing her to have her own way! Well things are about to change! You wait and see if they don't! When I see her I am going to find out just what she and that fellow have been up to!'

'I'm sure they weren't up to anything Brendon. Lucinda's a good girl, she wouldn't want to do anything to upset you dear; you know that!' cried Maggie, in a hopeless attempt to try to get her husband to calm down and to think again.

'There you go again, defending her! I checked her mobile phone only yesterday and there was a text on it from some boy asking her out! I expect it was him! I had hoped she'd have more sense than to answer it, but I was obviously wrong! Well, I shall get to the bottom of this, you mark my words; and I will confiscate that phone of hers and make sure she never lingers outside those school gates ever again! I'll drag her up the drive by her hair every day if she's going to behave like a whore!'

'Oh, wait till she's better, please Brendon! She'll need her phone to ring us while she's in hospital, in case she needs something!'

Just then Nurse Pitman popped her head around the door.

'We have your daughter settled on the ward, Mr Green. You can come and see her now. I'll show you where she is, if you'd like to follow me.'

'And about time too!' snapped Brendon as he grabbed his hat, before pushing his way past the startled nurse, almost knocking her off her feet. Margaret Green gave a weak, embarrassed little smile of apology and then bowed her head and scurried along after her husband.

71

Danny
Chapter 13

Danny spent the next few days worrying about Lucinda. He couldn't get her out of his mind. He spent his time constantly checking his mobile phone to see if she'd left him any messages. He felt confused and worried: what should he do? The video he'd taken of her on the morning of the accident had inadvertently shown her father pulling out into the traffic without looking. If he withheld it from the police, he would be concealing an important piece of evidence.

He was sure she must be as keen on him as he was on her; if not why had she asked him to go with her in the ambulance to the hospital? Questions kept flooding his brain, but he couldn't come up with any answers. If she liked him then why didn't she want to speak to him now? Why didn't she contact him? Perhaps her injuries were more severe than had first been thought. Perhaps she was dead! Although he felt sure the school would have informed them and they would have had a special memorial assembly or something if that had happened.

Eventually he plucked up courage to go and see the Headmaster.

'Good morning Sir. I'm sorry to bother you, but we're all keen to know if you've heard any news on Lucinda Green. We're all worried about her and no one seems to know anything.'

'I'm waiting for news myself Daniel,' replied Mr Hinton, the Head. 'I've heard nothing as yet. I promise I'll let you all know immediately any news becomes available. In the meantime I suggest no one worries too much, as no news is always good news.'

Danny wasn't so sure about that. He still found it impossible get Lucinda out of his mind and by the time his mother came home from work that evening he was so keyed up he felt as if he'd explode. As they sat together at the big pine kitchen table, eating spaghetti bolognaise, he asked her if she could think of any way to find out how Lucinda was.

Jennifer Stokes played with the spaghetti on her fork, searching for the right words, before finally looking up at her son.

'Danny, I realise you feel… close…' she said carefully, 'having been at the scene of the accident with Lucinda… and having accompanied her to the hospital… and it's obvious you'd like to know how she's getting on… but her father was clearly not comfortable with your presence Dan! Sadly, as unfair as it may seem to you, you must respect that and keep your distance my darling'.

'But Mum!'

'I'm sorry darling but I'm just telling it as it is. I spoke to your father on the telephone last night and told him how badly Lucinda's father had treated you at the hospital. He told me he is aware of this man … and he advises you to keep well away from him. Apparently he's a bit of a chancer. Your father doesn't want you to have anything more to do with him Dan. You must wait to find out how she is from the Headmaster or wait until she's well enough to come back to school. It isn't your business any more my darling.'

'But you don't know everything Mum!'

His mother put down her fork and frowned as she leaned forward across the table, 'What do you mean Danny?'

Danny got up and walked across to the sink to get a glass of water. He hesitated for a moment, trying to work out just how much information he should give his mother. He watched the water as it splashed inside his glass and sprayed out onto his jumper and then, with his face still turned away from her, he said sheepishly, 'I didn't tell the police everything Mum!'

'Danny?'

He then turned towards his mother, allowing his words to rush out.

'It was HIS fault Mum—it was her father's fault!'

'I think you'd better explain Dan,' replied his mother softly.

'He caused the accident—he drove out into the traffic without looking—he was responsible for all those people getting hurt! He drove out into the traffic without looking Mum—and I have evidence on my phone to prove it!'

He went back to the table and sat facing her.

'I didn't tell the police because I didn't want to upset Lucinda knowing the state she's in! How do you think she's going to feel knowing that her father has caused her pain?'

'I think you'd better begin at the beginning, don't you?' said his mother, gently laying her hand upon his. 'I think you'd better tell me everything Dan.'

For the next ten minutes Danny talked, relieved at last to get this burden off his chest and to allow his mother to take on the worries that had been torturing his mind during the last few days. When he'd finished Jennifer Stokes frowned, shook her head and took a deep breath before continuing.

'Oh, Danny, why didn't you tell me all this before? I realise you like this girl, but you really must stay away; you must stay away for your own sake! That father of hers seems to be a pretty nasty piece of work. I know you're worried for Lucinda but if you're not careful you'll be in real trouble yourself! The police don't like being led down the garden path Dan!' Jennifer picked up her plate as she got up from the table. 'I'll find out what I can.' She walked across to the sink, her face reflecting her concern. 'Hopefully the security camera outside school will also have picked up what you recorded—what you captured on your phone.' She crossed back to face her son. 'If not it's your duty to show the police what you have, and to act as a witness and give evidence if needed. You and I know you kept the information back to spare Lucinda's feelings, but you must also realise the police won't see it in the same way. I'll speak to your father again tomorrow; he may have more of an idea what to do. In the meantime—STAY AWAY!'

Danny spent the rest of the evening in his room with his ear-phones on, shutting out the world and its worries and allowing his music to wash over him. Later, as he lay in bed trying to sleep, he thought about Lucinda once more. He slept fitfully, her face being at the centre of all his dreams and by the time morning came he'd made a decision.

'Somehow I've got to find a way to speak to Lucinda. I don't care what Mum and Dad say. It's not her fault her father's a bad lot! I need to explain to her what happened, before she hears it from someone else'!

The next day was Friday and after lunch Danny excused himself from his history class saying he felt sick. He then headed for the hospital. When he arrived he lay in wait, until Lucinda's parents had emerged from the hospital entrance, and after he was sure they had driven away, he walked into the building and made his way up to her ward. By the time he'd reached it there was only five minutes left of visiting time and he rushed in, knowing this would be his only chance to see her alone.

'Hi Luce, how are you?'

'Danny! Dad didn't see you, did he?' She sounded terrified and he saw real fear in her eyes as she looked past him towards the door.

'No, don't worry I waited until I saw them drive off. I know he doesn't like me.'

'It's not just you Dan; he doesn't like seeing me talking to anyone! I'm not allowed friends outside school, especially boys.'

'Listen Luce, we haven't got long before the bell goes to end visiting, but there's something I really need to tell you,' he blurted out, not quite knowing how he was going to put what he had to say into words, or indeed how she was going to receive the information he was about to give her. In the end she took it fairly calmly and just nodded as she listened to him, showing no emotion. When he'd finished telling her what he'd seen and about the video he'd taken, she frowned, slowly shaking her head from side to side, trying to understand the implications of what she'd just been told. Then, with some resignation, she finally spoke.

'Yes, I remember.' She nodded slowly, her mind far away as she tried to visualise the moments before the accident. Then, her voice no more than a whisper, she said simply, 'I remember now. He was rushing to see someone about handing out hymn books in church on Sunday.'

'I'm so sorry Luce; I tried to keep it a secret from you! I didn't want you to know it was your father who'd put you in here, but Mum says I have to tell the police or else I'll be in real trouble.'

She nodded again to show her understanding.

'Perhaps it's time to tell the world Dan, so they can see him as he really is. Mum goes through hell and we both try to toe the line, so we don't upset him. We try so hard not to make him angry! He's so manipulative, he rules our life. He checks our phones each day to see if we've had a message or spoken to anyone. When he found your text, he was furious! He didn't say anything at the time, but I could see by his expression, by the set of his jaw that he'd seen it and I knew he'd use it against me or Mum in time. That's the way he is, the way he does things, he waits until the anger builds up inside him and then—he just explodes! That's why I never text you back.'

Just then the bell rang to indicate the end of visiting time.

'I'm sorry I put you in such an awful position Luce. I'd never have text you if I'd known what he was like. That's the bell so I've got to go. I don't know what's going happen next Luce. I just hope the security camera picked him up, then I may not have to say anything—but if not ......'

'Do what you have to do Dan, I understand—but please be careful. You don't know how angry he can get, and it's always poor Mum that suffers most! Try to get in to see me again if you can, to let me know what's happening, but don't let him see you. They usually leave here about ten minutes before the end of visiting time to miss the crush in the car park. Don't text or message me though because he'll see it. I won't say anything to anyone. I don't want to make things any worse for you than they already are.'

He nodded his understanding and smiled at her, and for a moment they held each other's gaze. Then he bent down and kissed her awkwardly on her cheek.

'Bye Luce see you soon,' he said shyly, before he turned quickly away and was gone.

She lay staring after him, her fingers touching the kiss, as if to hold onto it to keep it safe. She didn't want it to fly away.

Mary
Chapter 14

Propped up regally against her pillows Mary surveyed the ward she'd been incarcerated in now for two whole weeks. Although her wounds were slowly beginning to heal, she still looked as if she'd gone three rounds with Mike Tyson. She was feeling bored and had begun to worry how her office was running without her. No one had come to visit her; which she told herself was because they were all running round like headless chickens trying to cope. She would have liked to speak to someone about it; however, in her heart she knew she'd distanced herself from her staff for so long no one felt they knew her well enough, or even liked her enough to warrant a visit. Earlier experiences of hostility had made Mary determined not to allow personal relationships to become mixed up with office affairs. She believed to receive total respect you had to show them who was in charge, and if that needed to be done by using fear, then so be it!

Yesterday she'd telephoned her office to ask for work to be sent into her. It would lighten their load and, heaven forbid, she had plenty of time on her hands! She'd go mad lying around in here for another day without anything to do! But the office had told her *'everything was under their control'* and she *'mustn't worry about work as they were on top of it'*—and she felt... jealous! Jealous she was dispensable! They'd sent her an enormous basket of fruit (most of which would have gone off before she got around to eating it) but she could do without their gifts or their good wishes. What she really wanted was work; or at the very least to 'talk' to people about work. That was her life. That was all she knew!

She'd begged, but the doctors wouldn't allow her to leave hospital as *'she had no one at home to look after her.'*

'When,' she thought, 'have I ever had anyone at home to look after me? During my whole life I've never had anyone, so what's so different now?'

She half-heartedly picked up the magazine lying open at the foot of her bed; a magazine another patient had passed on to her. She put on the spectacles that were dangling from a chain around her neck, and reluctantly began to read about some brainless, rich pop idol that was getting a divorce from another equally brain-dead, rich pop idol.

'Bloody rubbish!' she muttered under her breath, 'Who the hell is interested in their sordid little lives? Who in their right mind would pay good money to buy this trash?'

'Good morning Mary how are you feeling today?' ventured Nurse Jones brightly.

Mary bristled at being called by her Christian name! At work she'd always insisted on being referred to by her surname 'Miss Parsons', and she found the familiarity extremely offensive.

'Is there anything you need this morning Mary?'

'A letter saying I can go home would be nice. I can't tell you how bored I am lying around in here with nothing to do!' replied Mary crossly.

'Well that's a good sign. It shows you're feeling better. The Doctor is on his rounds and should be with you shortly. Perhaps he'll have some good news for you.'

When the doctor did finally arrive, he examined her and declared she'd been very lucky and although it would take some time, her injuries would eventually heal, and she'd be left with no long-lasting damage. Then his face changed.

'Actually it's not your injuries that concern me Mary. I'm more concerned with your general physical state of health.' He paused and cleared his throat before continuing more seriously. 'I intend to be blunt with you! I'm not trying to frighten you, but it's my duty as your doctor to point out that if you don't do something about your weight very soon, then you could be dead within the next two years. Not only is it causing an enormous amount of strain upon your heart but you're also at serious risk of developing type 2 diabetes.'

Angered, Mary peered at him over her spectacles and looked him contemptuously up and down.

'It's very easy for you to say that Doctor,' she said equally seriously. 'Don't you think I've tried over the years? Do you really think I'm such an idiot that I enjoy looking like this? It's not so easy for some people to lose weight! We weren't all born to be stick insects!'

'I appreciate that Miss Parsons,' returned the slim doctor, as he too lowered his spectacles and peered over the top of them. With determined expression they each looked the other in the eye, and without breaking eye-contact, he removed his glasses and paused before speaking slowly and thoughtfully. 'If I were to recommend you as a suitable candidate for one of the new government health schemes, that are designed to help people just like you to lose weight, would you give it a try? Many people have found that by entering a controlled course of exercise and lifestyle change, motivation becomes easier. Would you be willing to give that a try? I'm prepared to refer you—but you would need to meet me half way. It's you that would have to do the hard work after all.' Silence hung between them before he continued. 'However, my warning is a serious one! What do you say?'

It took Mary a full minute to weigh up the doctor's words before she was able to make a reply. She then spoke quietly, without looking at him.

'Thank you Doctor, thank you for being so blunt, perhaps I needed that. It's very sobering to be told you have a death sentence hanging over you, particularly one that's been self-administered.' She paused again, and when at last she spoke it was with genuine emotion.

'I would like very much to take up your challenge Doctor—and I promise I will try my best to make your offer worthwhile.'

The doctor nodded, knowing full well how difficult it had been for his patient to absorb the news he had given her and to admit the fact her weight had become life-threatening and she really needed help.

After he'd gone Mary lay back deep in thought. She looked down at her bloated body and was repulsed by what she saw. She hated herself for having allowed it to happen. 'That is gross!' she thought. 'Mother was right.'

However, this time she wasn't left solely with self-loathing: this time she also had a little hope.

Valerie
Chapter 15

Val was still coming round from the anaesthetic when her husband, Ben, arrived at her bedside. She was still woozy after the operation to stabilise her spine. As he stood looking down at her drawn and pale face, he realised just how much he loved her and how devastated he'd be if anything happened to her. She'd been in hospital for a couple of weeks and had suffered so much pain that she'd been heavily sedated most of that time, meaning they were only able to have fragmented conversations. Ben had thought the last thing she'd want to talk about was the accident and so he'd carefully steered her away from the subject. However, at the back of his mind lingered so many unanswered questions—the main one being where had she been and who had she been with, while he'd been away? Although he desperately needed to know the answer, he was afraid to hear it—afraid her answer would somehow tear them apart.

After the accident, he'd rung her office to let them know what was happening. He'd asked if he could speak to one of the girls that had been on the London trip with her but no one had known anything about it! No one in the office had been up to London on that day. No one knew what he was talking about! He'd waited for her to explain. Waited for some clarification—but she avoided the subject or at least appeared too confused to remember where she had been. Ben was so anxious about her health that he didn't want to upset her by going on about it. But as he looked down at her now, his head was filled with so much doubt and uncertainty. Where had she been? Why had she lied to him? What had she got to hide?

Val stirred, and he stroked her hair and whispered, 'Its O.K. Val, I'm here.' Her eyes flickered, and when she opened them, she looked up at him and whispered, 'I'm sorry,' before closing them once again and floating back off to sleep. Ben stayed at her bedside for most of that day as she drifted in and out of consciousness, until she eventually came round and, although still weak, became more and more coherent.

'I've been trying to remember the accident Ben, but I'm so muddled and confused, I can't remember what really happened. I can remember skidding and then... seeing a bus coming towards me, but that's all. I think a car must have braked in front of me—it must have done in order to make me hit my brakes... but I'm not really sure. I remember an enormous bang... being hit from behind... and I think... spinning... but it's all a bit of a blur. It all happened so suddenly!'

'Don't worry about it now my love. You're confused from the anaesthetic. We need to get you better before you have to think about that. You gave me quite a shock you know. I was so scared I was going to lose you! Let's just think about getting you better; nothing else matters for now. You're sure to feel better in a few days' time, once the anaesthetic has worn off.' He kissed her forehead, and she smiled up at him. 'I had a word with your office, to let them know about the operation. They sent their love and told me to tell you to take off as much time as you need.' He looked down at her, searching her face, hoping she'd give him some explanation, some reassurance, but she just nodded and looked away.

''Oh shit!' she thought, 'He knows! He knows I wasn't out with the girls.' How she wished her head would clear. She couldn't think straight! She closed her eyes.

'I'll let you sleep now, my love. I'll come back again tomorrow morning.' He kissed her once more and squeezed her hand. 'I love you. Sleep well my darling.'

How much did he know? She couldn't sleep forever!

'Oh, shit!'

The next morning she felt better, well, a little anyway. At least her head was a bit clearer. The nurses were kind, and after they'd given her a bed bath and brushed her hair, she felt fresher and tidier. She was still lying flat on her back and would be for a little while yet, and each time she moved, even slightly, it hurt like hell, but she could at least 'feel', and the nurses told her that was a good sign.

At ten thirty Patrick's grinning face appeared at her bedside.

'Well hello there me darlin'! Aren't you the lazy one lying there! Well now, I told them I was your boss and that I had some get-well cards to cheer you up!' he said jovially. 'I said I was off to Ireland on business and I couldn't come at any other time, which was not all blarney; I do at least bring cards!' He chuckled at his little joke. 'I told them I'd only stay five minutes, so it's to be a flying visit I'm afraid me darlin'. I used the old Irish charm on the pretty little thing at the nurse's station. I'll be thinkin' your man might be comin' round later God help us, so I'll not be stayin' long!' He dropped a handful of cards onto the table across her bed.

'So, what did you tell him in order to cover up our little liaison eh?'

'Yes I'm fine thank you Patrick! Thank you so much for asking.' she uttered sarcastically.

'Sure you are! We'll not be keeping a fit girl like you down for long! So, what did you tell him then?'

Val let out an exasperated sigh. 'I've told him nothing—yet! Although I'm sure he knows I wasn't with the girls. I suppose I'm going to have to lie to him yet again!'

'You're a good girl to be sure you are. We don't want your little fling getting back to Alice now do we?'

'Oh no Patrick, we don't want your lovely wife to find out about your little flirtations, do we? Don't worry, I'll tell Ben he got it all wrong and I'd gone out with some girls from my previous job, friends I'd stayed in touch with. I'll ring them later and try to get one of them to cover for me, in case he tries to contact them.'

'Well I'd better be on my way me darling. The girls send their love, and Alice has sent some chocolates to cheer you up!' He laughed as he produced the chocolates from his coat pocket. 'We had ourselves some fun though didn't we me darlin', and we both know it wasn't meant to last.' His eyes twinkled. 'You were as keen as me to bring a little passion into your life girl. We both needed a little bit of something extra, so we did.' He grinned mischievously. The last time she'd seen that grin she'd been gazing into his eyes as they lay between the crisp white sheets in the hotel bedroom. Then it had made her stomach flip—now it just made her angry.

'I think it's better if I don't visit you again. We don't want Ben getting' any ideas, do we now?' He bent down and quickly placed an unemotional kiss upon her forehead. 'Get well soon now do you hear.' He flashed her one of his charming smiles once more, a well-practised smile designed to make anyone within his vicinity go weak at the knees, and then he turned quickly and headed for the door.

'You bloody little fool Val!' she said to herself as she watched him disappear. 'You knew from the outset there was never going to be anything in it—and yet you've risked everything for someone that doesn't care a damn!'

A few days later Ben, not able to contain his feelings any longer, finally plucked up courage to ask her where she'd been coming from on the day she'd had the accident. He thought he'd waited long enough for an explanation. Each day he'd hoped one would be forthcoming and each evening he'd drive home disappointed. When she did finally put forward the excuse she'd discussed with Patrick, the excuse she'd been rehearsing over and over again in her head every day since his visit, she knew in her heart that Ben didn't believe her, and she wondered if her marriage would ever be the same again.

Daisy
Chapter 16

When the day of her mother's funeral arrived, Daisy knew there was only one way she was going to be able to get through it and so, as the hearse drew up in front of her grandmother's front door, she closed her eyes for a moment and visualised being dressed in her beautiful gown of gold.

Before getting into the funeral car she raised her head defiantly and pictured lifting the hem of her skirt as she stepped into the beautiful gilded coach. It was pulled by two sleek black horses, decorated with white plumes. She took a deep breath and instead of thinking of her mother lying in the coffin as they followed the hearse, she imagined being taken to the Autumn Ball.

Everyone had been trying to persuade her she should say a few words or read a poem, or at the very least say a prayer for her mother during the service, but she was adamant she wouldn't and had stubbornly refused to do so. Why should she speak publicly? Her thoughts and memories were hers alone, locked away in her heart, not to be publicly displayed just so people could feel sorry for her. It had always been just her and her mother—a one parent family she'd heard people call it. Well, she had only ever wanted one parent! Her mother had been everything to her; they were friends as well as mother and daughter. She knew how much she loved her mother and she had no intention of sharing that love with anyone else! She wanted to hide away, to be allowed to remember her mother in her own way, to run from the pitying faces she'd already encountered and knew she would again before the day was over. How she wished she had died too!

She'd hardly spoken to anyone one all day, just a brief nod when kisses had been planted upon her cheek. But, as she followed her mother's coffin down the aisle of the church, she saw Tess standing in one of the pews and for a moment her heart soared. She knew in that moment everything was going to be alright and she'd be able to get through the proceedings, knowing Tess would be somewhere in the congregation standing behind her. Daisy had a feeling Tess, unlike most other people in the congregation, would understand exactly how she was feeling.

After the service, in the little room set aside for friends and relations to mingle and to drink tea, and eat sandwiches and fairy cakes, Daisy felt annoyed by the chatter and laughter going on about her. Her mother had just died and here they were having a party! It wasn't right! She looked around the Church Hall, her attention drawn to the pictures decorating the walls, no doubt done by children attending Sunday school. One picture in particular caught her eye. It was decorated with flowers and tiny animals and in the centre, the words 'Jesus loves us' was written in gold. She shook her head. How could that possibly be? If He had loved her He wouldn't have taken her mother away from her!

Suddenly she found Tess standing by her side, and they both stood looking up at the picture.

'Are you alright Daisy? It's a very unreal day isn't it?' Someone laughed behind them, and Tess watched Daisy turn around angrily. She put a steadying hand on the child's shoulder. 'It doesn't seem right to see people enjoying themselves, does it? People don't mean to be disrespectful; they just don't quite know how to behave or what to say, so it's easier for them to 'celebrate' your mother's life. Don't be angry with them. They mean well.'

Daisy looked up at Tess, who once again had understood exactly how she was feeling and what she was thinking.

'I hear you're going to live with your aunt, Daisy.'

'Yes.'

'I'm pleased about that; it'll be good for you to live with a family. Is that your aunt over there? I think she's looking for you.   I'd better let you go to her. You have my address Daisy. When you're settled will you write to me? I'd love to hear how you're getting on?'

Daisy nodded, unable to speak. How she wanted to stay by Tess's side but knew that wasn't possible and she must leave her. Without looking at Tess again, she turned to walk across to her aunt, but halfway stopped suddenly, and turned to give Tess a strange little smile. It was only then that Tess saw the fear in the child's eyes.

'No child should have to go through this,' she thought; as Daisy turned away again, and suddenly Tess had the saddest feeling she may never see innocence in that lovely young face ever again.

Daisy's life was in turmoil. It had been decided her grandmother wasn't fit enough to look after herself, let alone a twelve-year-old girl, and so Daisy's aunt had reluctantly agreed for her go and live with them after the funeral. She already had three children of her own, meaning their small house in Durham was about to become very over-crowded! Daisy was to share a bedroom with her fifteen-year-old cousin, Mattie. Mattie had not been at all happy about this and resented having to share her room with a 'baby'. Daisy was none too keen either; she'd always had her own room and had only met her cousin a few times anyway, as they lived miles apart. She felt like an intruder. She knew she wasn't welcome and each night, as she cried herself to sleep, she prayed for time to be turned back. She missed her mum so very much!

A fortnight after the funeral a letter dropped through Tess's letterbox.

"Dear Ms Matthews,

It was very kind of you to come to Mummy's funeral. It helped me to know you were sitting there. I'm now living with my aunt in Durham. It seems a very long way away. I try to be good as I know it's very kind of them to take me in. I share a bedroom with my cousin Mattie who is fifteen. I don't think she likes me very much and she's cross because she has to share her bedroom with me, but my aunt says we'll both have to make the best of it, as there's no more room in the house. I've started a new school. It's alright but not as grand as Linford School was and everyone teases me about my 'Southern' accent, but their accents are much funnier than mine! I can't understand them sometimes. I wish you were my teacher. I expect I'll get used to it, but it seems as if everyone here knows each other already and I feel a bit left out at the moment. I'm not very good at making new friends. Please, if you're not too busy, will you write back to me?

From Daisy"

Tess read and re-read Daisy's letter, searching between the lines for the child's true feelings, and by the end of the evening she'd carefully composed a letter to send back to her—and so began a series of letters that were to change both their lives forever.

Alan
Chapter 17

'I understand you were very brave Alan,' one of the nurses had told him that morning. 'I believe some people are only alive today because you put their pain before your own. You should be very proud of yourself.'

He certainly didn't feel brave—as far as he knew he had never been brave in his life! He didn't think that brave was in his nature—boring yes, but brave never. He felt confused; a fraud. How could something so totally life-changing become so easily forgotten? He couldn't even remember getting up on the morning it had happened—or catching the bus—let alone helping people. They'd told him the bus had crashed—but if that were true surely he'd remember!

'It's just your body shutting down while it tries to cope with the situation, that's all,' they told him, 'Your memory will return, but don't push it. It will come back when your body feels you're able to deal with it.'

Deal with it? Deal with what? Did they mean remembering the accident was going to be worse than losing a leg! How was he ever going to deal with that! How was he going to cope without a leg? Why couldn't he forget that! Why did that have to happen to him?

He'd never done anything to anybody! He didn't deserve it!

A feeling of hopelessness washed over him, dragging him into the bowels of despair as if a huge weight was pushing him downwards. He was unable to take it all in, unable to deal with his emotions right now. He couldn't even come to terms with the fact he'd only got one leg. What good was one leg? He found it so difficult to believe. It still felt as if he had two legs! He could still 'feel' two legs! The nurses had gone on about physiotherapy and exercise, as if that would make everything alright again. They'd talked of prosthetics— but they didn't tell him how he was going to be able to work again, to run for the bus, to climb the ladder when he had a leak in the roof—they didn't tell him how his life was going to change now he was legless!

He'd been staring at these walls now for weeks and he wasn't getting any better, he knew that. He didn't want to get any better. He didn't want to have to make the effort to get better. He didn't want to have to learn how to 'begin' again. So, day after day he lay there, staring at the walls, switching off, not wanting to think about the future, not wanting to come to terms with his loss. The nurses tried to cheer him up, but he found it so humiliating to have to accept help—help to do basic everyday things—things like going to the bathroom for a pee! He was a private individual, and proud: only failures accepted help.

He watched as other patients around him got better and one by one were allowed to leave the hospital and go home. One little girl had even come to his bedside with her parents, to bring him chocolates and to say goodbye and thank you. They'd said he'd bandaged the child's head, and he'd sung 'the wheels on the bus,' together with her as they'd waited to be cut out. They must have made it all up! He'd never sing such a silly, childish song—not ever—and certainly not in public! What the hell was going on, why was everyone lying, and if it was true, why couldn't he remember?

'It isn't fair!' he muttered 'Other patients are allowed to go home to their families, with their bodies intact, why can't I?'

To their families! He had no family! He knew his own elderly parents wouldn't come to take him home, how could they, they were so frail they couldn't even come to visit him—couldn't even look after themselves!

Alan had been born to elderly parents; his mother had been in her early-forties and his father fifty-three. When he came along, he must have come as a major shock to them! When he went to school the other children asked him if they were his grandparents and he became a creature of ridicule when they found out they were his parents. They made him feel ashamed, a feeling he would never be able to overcome and one that was to set him apart from the other pupils for the whole of his school life. How he had ever happened Alan could never fathom. They seemed so straight-laced, and the idea they had ever made love seemed impossible and slightly distasteful to him.

He'd been a child of the seventies, but his upbringing had been draconian. The rules of the house were: 'Always present yourself for inspection in a clean and tidy manner; shoes to shine at all times. Never answer back or you will get the cane. Play quietly; children should be seen and not heard. No hugs or shows of affection; they will only make you soft—if you fall over, get up and don't cry, crying is for babies!'

'They wouldn't think I looked too clean and tidy now,' he thought, 'but at least I'd only have to present one shoe for inspection!'

No, he had no one to turn to, no one at all! He lay there, expressionless, with hollow eyes open, looking out but seeing nothing. Some days he couldn't even be bothered to do that, and he'd lie there with his eyes closed, picturing nothing but blackness. Some days he couldn't be bothered to think. Some days he just couldn't be bothered at all.

Danny
Chapter 18

Geoffrey Stokes, Danny's father, finally arrived home from his American business trip. Although flying had become a necessary part and parcel of his job, he'd never quite got used to long-haul flights. Even though he flew first class, he could rarely sleep, and jet lag would dog him for days afterwards, making him feel tired and irritable.

'Your Mother tells me you've got yourself into a bit of a scrape over some young girl, Lad,' he asked his son bluntly after they'd adjourned to the lounge, while Geoff enjoyed a well-earned glass of single malt. 'I understand you've some evidence on your phone that the police may well be interested to see?'

'Yes, Dad' said Danny, beginning to feel self-conscious as his father's unsmiling face looked across at him. Although in awe of his father, Danny always felt uncomfortable talking to him. His father had, he knew, a brilliant mind and having a conversation with him only made Danny feel inadequate and stupid. Whatever he said always came out sounding silly and childish.

'So what do you intend doing about it?' continued his father offhandedly.

'I really don't know. I was hoping you might be able to suggest something Dad?'

Danny sat awkwardly on the edge of his seat waiting for his father's reply, while Geoff sat looking thoughtfully at the whiskey he was swirling around in his glass. He then took a swig, before leaning forward towards his son, his stern expression telling Dan that he was in for a difficult time. His piercing eyes held Dan's for a moment before he answered.

'I 'suggest' the first you do is to get this stupid, teenage idea about being in love out of your head!'

Immediately Danny was tongue-tied and felt idiotic, which was exactly the effect Geoffrey Stokes had hoped to achieve.

'Then you go down to the police station and show them what you've got recorded on your mobile phone— and hope to god they'll understand why you hadn't taken it in sooner!'

Danny looked worried. 'It's been difficult Dad. Her father's really aggressive and manipulative. She's frightened he might turn nasty and hit her mum!'

'That's all the more reason for you to keep out of it and to let the police handle it!'

'It's not as easy as that Dad! I can't walk away and let her deal with it on her own. She's got no one else to turn to! I'll do what I need to do as far as the police are concerned but there's no way I'll stop supporting her!'

'And what do you hope to achieve by 'supporting' her? Has she asked you to become involved? How do you think her father will feel knowing you've been instrumental in getting him convicted of dangerous driving? Do you think that will help her? Do you think he'll allow you to see her after that?'

'All I know is that both she and her mother need help!'

'But they haven't asked for your help Daniel!' said Geoffrey Stokes, raising his voice and emphasising every single word. 'You have taken this upon your own shoulders—and you'll most likely cause them more trouble by pursuing it! Don't you realise all you're doing is making a difficult situation even worse for her!'

'So, are you telling me to sit back and do nothing? To let it happen! To let him hurt her?'

Danny's father, exasperated by his son's argumentative attitude, slammed his glass down upon the coffee table and shouted, 'No boy that is not what I am suggesting! What I'm suggesting is you take what you know to the police and let them decide! It is not the responsibility of a seventeen-year-old boy to do their work for them!'

Father and son held eye contact, each daring the other to break first; never before had Danny dared to confront his father. Tension hung between them as they glared at each other. Realising his son wasn't going to accept his advice, Geoff eventually picked up his glass and sat back, looking down into the amber liquid, as if searching for inspiration. Eventually he looked up again and spoke to his son very quietly.

'Do you realise how difficult this 'supporting her' would become in our life, your mother's and mine? No? I suspect that's never entered your head, has it boy?'

Without taking his eyes away from Danny, Geoff drained what was left in his whiskey glass and stood up.

Danny frowned, 'Your lives?'

Geoff walked over to the fireplace where he put his empty glass down upon the mantelpiece.

'Is this the thanks we get for sending you to a good school, for having to work all the hours that God sends in order to pay the extortionate fees it takes to put you there?'

Danny looked away, not sure how to respond.

'Do you realise how a scandal like this would affect my position? I'm a respected Member of Parliament. I have to prove every day that I'm squeaky clean. Can you imagine how it would appear on the front page when the tabloids picked up the story that my son had withheld evidence—because of the love of some girl? Do you really want to rock that boat? Do you really want to risk me losing my job because of 'some girl'? Because if you do, it wouldn't be just me that would be affected, you would have to leave that posh school of yours, and we would all have to leave… this…' he waved his arms in the air to indicate their grand home, with its expensive furniture. 'It doesn't pay for itself you know!'

Danny sat head down, looking at his feet. He then, without warning suddenly jumped up and faced his father.

'I used to be in awe of you Dad, always trying to help people and to do the right thing by them. You taught me that! I think perhaps you might have lost touch. Your expensive life style seems to have become part of you now. I want to help someone, and yes maybe it will reflect badly on us all, who knows? But Lucinda needs help, and her mother needs help, and I'm going to try to give them that help. If I have to do that without your blessing, well so be it.' Then he smiled, 'I'm sorry Dad, I don't mean to be disrespectful, but you can only blame yourself—after all it's just the way you brought me up.'

Danny turned and left the room and Geoff stared, speechless, after him. He stood for a while, staring at the closed door. Was Danny right? Had he become so used to the affluent lifestyle his world now afforded him, that he'd become insensitive to those whom he had once wished to help?

He stood there, thinking back to his earlier days, when he had fire in his belly and he'd speak out for injustice. In those days he wouldn't have been afraid to speak his mind, to upset anyone, as long as he thought his cause was right and worth fighting for. He was shocked to realise that his son could be right. Had he really changed so much without even recognising it? Had a seventeen year old boy just put him in his place?

Eventually the door opened halting his reverie and his wife entered the room.

'Is everything alright, Love? Did I hear raised voices?'

Geoff smiled as he put his arm around his wife's shoulders. 'I think I've just been hauled over the coals Jen. I do believe our son is growing up!'

Tess
Chapter 19

Tess, the middle and most boisterous child of three, always appeared happy and much preferred climbing trees with her older brother and his friends, than she did playing with her dolls. She was a pretty little thing with short, coal black, curly hair, which she hated... She longed to have long, straight hair like her sister but unfortunately she'd taken after her father's side of the family, where curls were the order of the day. They would knot and tangle when allowed to get out of control, causing shrieks and squeals every morning before school, as her mother tried to tame them! In an attempt to avoid these morning fracases, her mother decided that the only way to promote peace and harmony in the home was to have her hair cut very short, much to the indignation of Tess. Tess had also inherited her father's dark brown eyes, which often twinkled in a most mischievous manner and became a tell-tale sign when she was up to no good.

Next to climbing trees her passion had been dancing. She rarely stood still and twirled and pirouetted around the house at great speed, inevitably knocking over one of her exasperated mother's precious ornaments, resulting in her being sent to her room. So often did this occur that, when taken to visit one of her aunt's, she would be lectured for days before they went and told she must "sit still in a chair at all times, until it was time for them to go home!" This was purgatory for young Tess. She longed to explore the garden, to roll on their manicured lawn, or to play hide and seek with her brother in and out of the bushes.

Her sister—her long, straight haired, beautiful sister—was everything Tess wasn't. She would smile and sit primly, with her hands in her lap, never spilling her drink or dropping biscuit crumbs down her pretty dress and people would compliment her on her perfect manners. Tess felt so unlike her sister that she often wondered if she'd been adopted, she'd even put this question to her mother one day.

"Good gracious child, what on earth made you think that? Of course you weren't adopted; you only have to look at your father to see that. You're the image of him. Don't worry darling, one day you'll learn to become an impeccable young lady just like your sister!"

That annoyed Tess even more. She didn't want to become like her sister, like her boring, butter wouldn't melt in the mouth sister—no way!

Eventually, on the advice of her teacher (who had found it a challenge to keep Tess contained in her seat for a whole lesson), it was decided she would be enrolled for dance and drama classes, in an attempt to rein in and to give a controlled outlet for her physical needs. It was indeed just what Tess needed, and she enjoyed the classes enormously. Here she could twirl and pirouette just as much as she liked, and it wasn't long before she'd become extremely good at both subjects and had passed all her examinations with flying colours.

When she left school she went on to a teacher training college, and although still lively and full of exuberance, she became slightly more self-restrained. Nevertheless, she was still the life and soul of the student house where she lodged and was given the nickname 'Tess the Tornado'! During her time at college, she met and fell in love with fellow teacher-to-be, Paul Matthews. He was a quiet young man who was attracted to Tess's high-spirited ways. Once they'd both graduated it seemed inevitable, after finding suitable employment, their next step would be to get married.

Their wedding took place on a lovely day at the end of July and as the sun shone down upon them they thought themselves the luckiest couple on earth. Tess looked so lovely in her long white, full skirted wedding gown, with a headdress of tiny red roses secured over her black curls.

'You look so beautiful," Paul had told her, 'you remind me of Snow White.'

Tess had laughed as she looked across at the family group assembled ready for their photograph.

'So, which of our mothers do you think will play the role of the Evil Queen?' she'd whispered in his ear.

They both found work very quickly, in different schools, but within striking distance of each other, which meant they were able to travel to and from work together. Occasionally one or the other would have to stay behind to run after-school clubs. Tess had started a new drama club at her school. It took up a lot of her time, but she was eager for it to succeed. Once a year she put on a show for pupils and parents to attend and it became a much-anticipated event in the school calendar.

After four ecstatically happy years, Tess became pregnant, and both she and Paul were overjoyed! They loved children, and this seemed to be the most natural course of events to seal their happiness. She'd take maternity leave for a year, and afterwards they'd find a suitable baby minder, until the child was old enough to go to pre-school. Paul's mother had offered to look after the baby for two days a week, so there'd only be three days left to pay for child care.

Throughout her pregnancy Tess was plagued by high blood pressure and was confined to bed several times, which was purgatory for lively Tess. She couldn't wait for her life to get back to normal—or whatever normal was to be with a new baby in tow.

Eventually, after nine long and worrying months, she finally went into labour. However, this too was to be eventful as Tess wasn't allowed the natural birth she had hoped. Because of complications, the baby had to be delivered into the world, via a C-section, under general anaesthetic.

When she eventually came round from the anaesthetic, she could see Paul looking totally exhausted and extremely anxious—but when her beautiful baby was put into her arms for the first time, she felt an immediate bond. A warm surge of love, unlike anything she'd experienced before, took over her whole body and any concerns she may have had just evaporated.

'Congratulations, you have a beautiful, healthy baby daughter Mrs Matthews,' announced the doctor as he stood looking affectionately at mother and child. His face then changed to one of concern as he continued softly, 'but I fear I'm also the bearer of bad news my dear.'

Tess turned to look at Paul, once again seeing his worried expression, and she reached out her hand to him, knowing she wasn't going to like whatever she was about to hear.

'Because you experienced such a difficult birth, Mrs Matthews, I'm afraid, in order to save your life, we had to give you a hysterectomy after she was delivered— you won't be able to have any more children I'm afraid.'

'We have one perfect little girl Tess, let's just be thankful for that.' butted in Paul, who'd already been informed and had planned his response to her. He squeezed her hand and smiled down at her. 'The doctors have been amazing Tess! They saved your life.' He kissed her forehead, and she then realised what a dreadful ordeal he'd been through as she saw the tears that welled in his eyes.

Tess nodded. 'But we wanted a large family Paul. That won't be possible anymore! This little one will never have a brother or sister to play with!'

'Let's give thanks for what we have Tess. It'll mean we can lavish all our love and attention on her. We'll be able to afford to give her the very best things in life!'

And they did! They named her Eleanor, Ellie for short, and she became the love of their lives. The three of them a tightknit group of love and laughter. Ellie was a clever little girl. She did well at school academically and passed to go to Grammar School. She also excelled in both music and sport, playing the piano and becoming a fine swimmer. It seemed as if Ellie could do no wrong and one day she'd be able to become whatever she wanted—and whatever that was she'd excel in it. All her parents wished was that she'd always be as happy as she was now.

In July, just before she was due to begin her new school, Tess and Paul took her on holiday to Cornwall. This also coincided with their fifteenth wedding anniversary and they were all looking forward to it enormously. They'd chosen Cornwall as Ellie and Paul had wanted to try their hand at body boarding. Tess preferred to relax in the sun with a good book after a busy school year, which had ended with her usual annual school production. Once again it had been heralded an enormous success, the best production to date. The responsibility, however, for after-school rehearsals, sorting out costumes, making sure everyone knew their lines and came in at the right time and in the right place had exhausted her. Added to that the interminable school reports she'd had to write and Ellie's school commitments—made her feel she'd earned her reward to lie in the sun.

The weather was perfect as Tess lay on her sun-bed reading, dozing and daydreaming, as the sun shone down and relaxed her tired body. As she lay back and looked up at the cornflower blue sky, she smiled as she imagined the shape of a teddy bear in the fluffy white clouds above her. She hoped it would stay long enough to show Ellie when she came back out of the sea but knew it would be unlikely. She felt a warm glow inside as she thought of Paul and Ellie bonding as they splashed about in the water, practising their new-found sport.

Both Paul and Ellie were extremely competitive, always trying their best to outdo each other at whatever sport they played. They took the waves on their brand-new body boards, both laughing and egging each other on, pushing themselves to do better and better each time, trying to find waves to take them further than the last.

Paul had just taken an amazing wave and he looked back to see if Ellie had seen how far he'd come. He realised immediately she was in trouble! He tried his best to swim out to her, but a riptide current held her in its power and kept taking her further away from him. He could see her struggling to swim back against it, but it was hopeless, and she was becoming more and more exhausted as it took her further and further out! She began to splash about wildly in panic, trying to fight with the current; and try as he might he was powerless to help her! He shouted, he screamed her name, he yelled for help from nearby swimmers, who also tried to swim out to her—but Paul could only watch as his daughter, his beautiful, beautiful daughter, his life, was swallowed up by the sea.

Tess heard the commotion from the shore and leapt up to see what was happening as people rushed past her running down towards the water.

'What's the problem,' she shouted to one of them.

'Someone in trouble in the water, I think.' came the reply.

'Dear God, don't let it be them, please don't let it be them,' she thought.

She ran frantically, stumbling in the sand to the edge of the water where it soon became apparent to her. She could see Paul, she could hear him yelling—but Ellie was nowhere to be seen.

The lifeguards brought her lifeless little body back to the beach. They tried and tried, first with CPR and then, when the equipment arrived, with a defibrillator but it was all over by then—Ellie had gone.

Paul was distraught. 'I tried to reach her Tess! I tried to reach her—but the current was too strong, it just carried her further and further away from me! I'm sorry Ellie—I'm so sorry!' and he dropped to his knees as he broke down sobbing into the sand.

Suddenly Tess felt an explosion inside her head! How dare he? How dare he? He allowed this to happen! She just looked at him. She was so angry. Why? Why hadn't he been looking after her? That was his job— that's what fathers do: keep their children safe! She could only feel contempt as she looked at his pathetic figure lying face down in the sand, and instead of going to him, she turned her back on him and walked slowly back up the beach.

She felt very little after that. She could vaguely remember the funeral, the small white coffin and the wildflowers, and people with tear-stained faces hugging her, but that was about all. She was numb, not sad, not crying, not feeling anything, just numb.

She and Paul drifted after that, each wading through their own tide of emotion, each being dragged in a different direction. They began avoiding each other. Paul would spend longer than needed at the office; anything was better than to go home and face the silence. Their sex life became extinct—they could barely look at each other let alone have physical contact. Their conversations, the silly little remarks they used to enjoy, were now meaningless. Ellie was never discussed—a taboo subject—seemingly unremembered—and yet at the heart of everything that was left unsaid. Paul became more and more submerged in his own pitiful world, unable to cope with his guilt and for a time he went off the rails and drank heavily, picking up with any girl that was willing to give him the temporary outlet he craved— anything to blot out his nightmares.

Tess merely isolated herself until her friends gradually retreated. They'd used up all their platitudes. Those with children no longer had anything in common with her and moved away. They didn't mean to be unkind, they just didn't know how to help, and Tess neither noticed, nor cared about anything.

One night when Paul arrived home from work he found her sitting on the floor in a darkened room facing a blank wall, rocking back and forth, totally expressionless. He realised then she needed help—realised they both needed help and could go on no longer the way they were, so he called for an ambulance. Tess was diagnosed as having suffered a total breakdown, and she was taken into a psychiatric clinic, where she stayed for the next five months.

Their marriage finally broke down. Ellie had gone, and when they were together it only underlined their loss. The three had become two, and neither of them could ignore the empty chair that sat staring at them. They were meant to be a three, and it could never be the same between them again. Their relationship had been built on happiness, and there was no room in it for heartache.

When Tess was allowed home from the clinic, she wasn't totally recovered. She looked rested and people hugged her and told her how well she looked and offered her platitudes that time would heal. However, she knew that time would never heal, it may scab over, but it would never heal. She was still grieving, but at least now she could 'feel' the grief which, she supposed, was a step in the right direction. She continued to attend counselling sessions, although she didn't feel they helped—how could someone who had never gone through the things she had gone through know how she felt?

Six years after Ellie's death and still hurting, but knowing she at least had to try to move on, Tess decided she'd retrain as a teacher. Her divorce had, at last, come through, and she'd heard that Paul was seeing someone else and intending to marry again. She was happy for him; she knew he'd never make it alone. She also knew she needed to work, both for the money and for some form of distraction and that was when she found herself teaching drama in the bowels of Linford School and where she met Daisy—Daisy who reminded her of her daughter—Daisy who was to become her new life.

Mary
Chapter 20

Mary hadn't always been fat. For the first few years of her life, she'd been a sweet little thing—but that was before her father's cuddles had turned into something else, before he'd become abusive to her and before Mary had felt the need to find comfort in eating. Try as she might she couldn't wipe from her memory the sound of his footsteps on the stairs as he arrived home late at night, drunk from the pub. She would clutch the bedclothes tightly about her and wait in terror to hear which bedroom door he would finally stop at and open— her mother's or her own.

He'd told her 'it was their little secret' and if she mentioned it to another soul she'd be extremely sorry because no one would believe her. They'd think her a dirty little slut for saying such disgusting things. He said the only reason he did it was because he loved her and no one else would want her—and so Mary suffered his foul words and his beer smelling breath and his dirty, sweaty hands pawing all over her body for more than ten years, until the day he finally died. She was never sure if her mother knew what he was doing to her and she was too frightened and ashamed to ask—but on the day she was told he'd been knocked down and killed in a hit and run car accident while walking home from the pub, all she could think was 'GOOD!' At least he would no longer creep into her bed at night and she wouldn't have to smell his stinking breath! After his funeral, attended by only a handful of people, most of them smelling of alcohol, he was never spoken of again, at least not to her.

At school, she was shunned. Her nickname, 'Fatty Parsons from the council estate', would be chanted over and over again. Children would lie in wait behind a wall as she walked home alone from school, ready to throw rotten vegetables at her or pour dirty water over her. She became the school's target of amusement—and when she arrived home in a disgusting state after one of these ambushes, her mother would say it was her own fault for being such a dirty, fat cow and that she'd brought it upon herself.

By the time she was seventeen, she had weighed well over twenty stones. Her mother told her she was gross, and she was an embarrassment to her, and instead of the love that Mary craved she just suffered more hostility and more guilt—and so she ate more food.

When Mary finally left school with eight GCSE's, no one was particularly surprised. She never went out and her studies had become her only escape. Of course, she had no praise for her accomplishment from her loving mother, who saw it as 'a useless piece of paper, as no one would employ a dirty, fat, useless slug-like her anyway'. Unfortunately, she was right as Mary had found it very difficult to find work—at least well-paid work, suited to her qualifications. She got plenty of interviews, but as soon as she walked in to face their questions and they saw her enormous size, she was immediately turned down, and the job given to some pretty little thing without any brains. She was destined to be pushed away in some back office, sorting out their inevitable problems while receiving only half their wage. As her mother had told her, she was an embarrassment to everyone and she came to believe she was right. Although competent at whatever was thrown at her, she found it hard to find work that satisfied her, as she applied for job after job after job without success.

Eventually, after several years and much perseverance, she got the job at Newman & Co. Solicitors, as their senior Legal Secretary and she was delighted. For a time, it had even encouraged her to diet—but that didn't last long, as loneliness soon forced her back into her old ways—what else do you do in the evening with nowhere to go and no friends to go with, but eat?

Once her mother had died she moved out of the council house she'd lived in all her life and bought a little terraced house of her own. Here she felt more content and was able to gradually put behind her the lurid memories of her old home, which had so constantly plagued her. Her new home had a small walled garden, where she grew lettuce and carrots—and she inherited a cat, who became her constant companion. They both seemed to recognise that nobody else wanted them and, as long as neither asked for any affection, they got along just fine.

Mary never went out socially and the only conversation she'd have all day was when one terrified little office girl plucked up courage to bravely venture into her domain, asking advice on some problem she'd been unable to sort out alone. This rarely happened, as girls who'd lain awake at night, would go to great lengths to find an answer before this drastic measure needed to be taken. Behind closed doors, Mary was still the companies laughing stock—but her position gave her a measure of respect. As she was the one doing the hiring and firing, laughter at her expense was kept to a whisper—and then only in the pub after work, nervously looking over their shoulders, just in case she should appear!

Life was to change quite dramatically for her after the crash though.

Once she'd been discharged from the hospital she went back to work as soon as she could—possibly too soon—but sitting looking at four walls, with only Tabatha for company, was not her idea of fun.

Then one day, when she arrived home from work, she found the referral letter to the gym her consultant had suggested, on her doormat and when she read it her stomach turned over! How she dreaded that first appointment! What would they think of her?

I expect I'll get some eighteen-year-old blonde bimbo, who'll take one look at me before running for cover in the opposite direction!' she mused, and as she imagined the scene she chuckled to herself, as she polished off yet another Mars Bar. 'They don't know what they're in for. I'll make mincemeat of them! If they expect me to do press ups, eat like a sparrow and be down to nine stone in two weeks then they've got their work cut out!'

Her first appointment did, however, surprise her. Firstly, it wasn't an eighteen-year-old blonde bimbo at all, but a fifty-something skinny little man with Persil-white teeth. No problem, she could deal with him! In fact, she would quite enjoy taking that whiter than white smile off his silly little face!

'Right, Mary, may I call you Mary?' Frank said jauntily while looking down at the notes that the hospital had sent him.

'My name is Miss Parsons,' came her threatening reply.

'OK'. He paused as he looked up from her notes, before continuing in a more respectful mode. 'Right, "Miss Parsons", my name is Frank Fielding, and it is my pleasure to meet you. I hope that we'll soon become good friends and that you'll feel in much better health after you've become familiar with our workouts.'

'Workouts, Sir? You don't expect me to lie on the floor and do pelvic thrusts, do you? I doubt I'll ever get down onto the floor and if I do I certainly won't be able to get up again! So, unless you feel like doing some heavy lifting, which you don't appear capable of, I should curb your enthusiasm!'

Frank smiled, 'I don't quite know what you are expecting 'Miss Parsons', however, that was the last thing on my mind. I thought today we'd just go over what we can do to help you. First, I must congratulate you. It's very brave of you to come here to see us.'

'Brave! What's brave about it?' she snapped at him. 'I suggest it is you who will need to be brave and not me!'

He smiled again. Damn it; she was getting fed up with that self-satisfied smile. When would the silly little man take that smirk off his face?

'Well I understand you've been in hospital Miss Parsons. Its brave, I thought, that you should come and see me so soon after lying in bed for a month, having had no exercise. That can't have been easy for you. Anyway, humour me, let's just run through my charts and decide how I can best help you, and indeed if you want my help. This is very much a two-way process Miss Parsons, and you can drop out at any time you like,' he smiled once more and, after a momentary pause, continued, 'as indeed can I.'

Ah, the pearly king is trying to annoy me, she thought, He wants me to drop out. He probably sees me as an impossible case and can't bear the thought of failing! Well I'm not going to make life that easy for him. He can jolly well work for his money!

The first thing the 'pearly king' addressed was Mary's lifestyle: at home, at work and at play. He asked her when she took exercise—or in her case when she didn't! They talked about how she could exercise even though she was sitting behind an office desk all day.

'You'll be asking me to go for a jog around the block in my lunch break next!' she barked at him.

He held up his hand. 'Oh heaven forbid Miss Parsons; I don't think you're ready for black Lycra yet!'

Damn him, whatever she said he could top it!

He then turned his discussion to her food intake, what she ate and when and where she ate it. He frowned when she told him about the convenience foods she bought on the way home from work.

'I think I'd better give you a few recipes Miss Parsons' He held up a finger. 'Don't worry I don't intend to starve you—yet. I do intend though, to make sure you follow a more nutritious and less calorific lifestyle from now on.'

'Don't you worry sir, I have no intention of allowing you starve me!' she bit back.

'Well, let's take it a step at a time, shall we?' he replied with yet another grin, 'I'm looking forward to this challenge Miss Parsons. I hope that you are too.'

'Huh!' she grunted. There was that self-satisfied smile again! He's just finding this one big joke, she thought. Well, I'll show you who's going to have the last laugh, you horrible little man!

'I think that's about enough for one day Miss Parsons. I'll work out a plan of action for you, and I shall look forward to seeing you again at the same time next week.' He stood up and offered her his hand.

'What! I've only been here for five minutes! We haven't done anything yet!'

Frank smiled again. 'It's been nice to meet you and to get to know you Miss Parsons. I'm sure we're going to have great fun together.'

'Huh!' she replied as she heaved herself out of the chair ignoring his hand, 'We'll see!' she said as she waddled off towards the door.

'We will indeed,' he said to himself after the door had closed behind her. 'I think I may have a fight on my hands here. I might just wait a while before I begin her exercises; in another week or so she'll be begging me to allow her to go on the walking machine! What a challenge!' He then went about writing his plan. 'I must go gently with this one, but I think the way forward is to treat it as a challenge. I think that our Miss Parsons enjoys a good fight!'

Alan
Chapter 21

Alan was the last of the crash victims to be left in the hospital and gradually, over time, his memory and his outlook on life began to improve. He was doing well in the gym and was gradually becoming more confident when using his prosthetic limb. He realised he was stronger and more determined than he'd thought himself capable and was proud of how he was managing to deal with his adversity. Once his clouds of despair had lifted, he'd been determined to show everyone how hard he could work to get better, or maybe it was how hard the hospital physiotherapists and occupational therapists had made him work, in order to get him back onto his feet again. Every day he'd go down to the gym to work out, and every day he'd feel some slight improvement, both physically and mentally.

He'd been given his own wheelchair and was now expert at using a banana board to help him get from his bed and into his chair without any mishap. Although there had been one occasion when he hadn't the patience to wait for the help of a nurse, and had ended up in an undignified heap upon the floor having to endure yet another telling off from Nurse Jones! Despite that he'd remained determined and had now mastered the art, meaning he needed to wait for no one and could get around the hospital with ease. Suddenly he was in charge of his life once more. He could do things for himself without waiting for a nurse to become available. He'd become independent and could get into the lift unaided. He could take himself down to the hospital shop whenever he wanted to buy a newspaper. He could buy a bottle of orange juice when he wanted a change from hospital water. It wasn't that he really needed these things, but the joy of feeling in control of his own destiny again gave him a reason for living. It had been a long, hard slog but he was beginning to realise he could overcome situations that once seemed impossible and was excited by the challenge of finding methods to conquer obstacles in his way.

He'd made friends in the gym, friends who'd also lost one or both of their limbs, friends who were encouraging him to take part in wheelchair basketball, friends he'd things in common with! He 'fitted in', something he'd never experienced before, he was 'one of them'. Sport had never been his thing, or so he'd been led to believe. Now he was being told he was 'a natural'! He'd never before had friends who wanted him; who wanted him to play on their team. At school, he'd always been the last one chosen. Now they were suggesting once he went home, he should apply to the Great Britain Wheelchair Basketball Association!

Ah! Home! Whilst most patients yearned to be allowed to go home; Alan dreaded it! The thought of once again being shut away in his own home, his dungeon, scared the hell out of him. He knew he was almost ready to go, and it wouldn't be long before the doctor signed his release. Although he'd been fully prepared by the nurses to look after himself, what they couldn't prepare him for was the loneliness—long dark evenings, sitting in front of the tele with no one to talk to. He pictured what life had been like before his accident and remembered the days he'd go without speaking to a soul—not properly speaking, not a conversation. Not days like this, when he'd laugh, make jokes and feel relaxed. He knew once he got home and closed the front door he'd be entering his lonely, silent world again, and he was petrified.

Here he knew everyone. He knew all the nurses by their Christion names. He knew when they clocked on and off. He knew about their families and their boyfriends and where they were going on their days off. He knew when the consultants would be doing their rounds and he knew the lads down in the gym—his mates! The hospital had become his new home and he didn't want to go back to the old one he'd left behind. He even voiced his fears to Nurse 'Joyce', as he called his favourite nurse.

'It's only natural for you to feel like this, Alan' she said sympathetically one morning, after he'd spent a sleepless night worrying about it and felt the need to speak to someone about his fears. 'You've been with us for a long time, and you've got to know us all so well— and we have got to know and love you too! We'll miss you as much as you'll miss us! But you'll come back to visit us won't you, when you come back for your check-ups? You jolly well better anyway, or you'll have me to answer to!'

Nurse Jones laughed the kind of laugh that makes you feel all is well with the world.

'When you've been home for a week or two you'll wonder why you ever thought like this. You're more than capable of getting around on your own now—and you'll be referred to all sorts of things to keep you busy! I'm told you're good at wheelchair basketball! You'll find you'll hardly have time to give us a second thought!'

Alan smiled and nodded but he knew as soon as he was allowed to go home he'd go back to his old ways. You can't teach old dogs new tricks! It all sounded so easy but he knew he'd never be able to walk into a new group of people. The whole idea of that already filled him with dread. He knew in his heart he'd open his front door, switch on the tele and not see another soul until he came in for his next appointment—and that filled Alan with total despair.

Lucinda
Chapter 22

Most people thought Lucinda's father annoying, yet to some degree he was also respected in the community. He was reliable and got things done. No one particularly wanted to spend more time than needed in his presence, but it was appreciated he was the person to contact whenever anything needed organising. He didn't so much ask people to become involved, he'd be more likely to bully them into submission, until they found themselves doing jobs they'd have preferred not to have become involved in. Although certainly not someone to cross, and not particularly liked, he was nevertheless thought harmless. No one ever envisaged the cruel, conniving person that lurked beneath *his bonne homme* facade.

Only Lucinda and her mother knew the real man, the one they lived in fear and dread of upsetting ,and the one that took great care to conceal his viciousness behind his closed front door.

Lucinda had been home from hospital for a week and, as far as she knew, no one had contacted him about causing the crash. If they had she thought she'd have known by his attitude, he certainly wouldn't have been able to keep his temper to himself. Perhaps Danny had been wrong.

The hospital had advised her to convalesce for a while before going back to school, which meant she hadn't been able to see Danny, and she hated not knowing what was going on. Her father had kept a strict eye on her since her return home and had confiscated her mobile phone. Not that it had made a great deal of difference, knowing he'd be monitoring her calls made it quite impossible to contact anyone anyway. Her mother kept telling her he'd soon get over his 'bad patch' and to just 'be a good girl until he's calmed down'.

It was always like this. Whenever one of his vicious moods took hold of him they both lived in terror, as much for each other as for themselves, until he'd worked it out of his system and forgiven them.

'Mum, we've done nothing wrong! We've got nothing to be forgiven for! None of this is our fault!'

'I know love, but you know how he is, he'll come around eventually.'

'And while we wait for that, you continue to get knocked about Mum! I've heard it—you and him, fighting—and I've seen the bruises you can't quite get your make-up to cover. Mum, I'm frightened! You need to get help before he does something really serious to you!'

'No love, leave it. He doesn't mean it—doesn't mean to hurt me, he's always really sorry afterwards. I can take it, as long as he doesn't hurt you.'

'We need to get away from him Mum, can't you see that?'

'But where to Lucinda, where could we go to? I have no money. Whatever I earn he takes off me, 'to put away for a rainy day' he says. We have nowhere to go love.'

'He takes the money off you Mum for exactly that reason, so he can control you, so you'll feel indebted to him! He knows only too well you'd be too frightened to leave him! He's manipulated you for so long that he's brainwashed you into thinking you need him more than you really do!'

'Leave it Lucinda. Please, leave it. I know what I'm doing!' insisted Maggie. 'We really do need him love—and he can be really sweet sometimes; particularly when he feels he's helping someone.'

Lucinda was angry at her mother's reluctance to accept there was something wrong. Of course she should leave him, and if she didn't do it soon Lucinda feared it would be too late! She'd heard them arguing ever since she'd been home from hospital—at least she'd heard him, ranting and raving downstairs in the living room, until she could bear it no longer and was forced to put her head under the covers to shut out the sound. She hated feeling so helpless but knew if she tried to interfere it would only make things worse for her mother. She'd seen the bruises reflected in their dressing table mirror as she went past their bedroom door that morning. It wasn't the first time she'd witnessed them either and each time they seemed to be getting a little worse. She really feared for her mother's life! While she'd been in the hospital she'd heard her mother telling someone she'd 'fallen over and hit her head while carrying the washing down the stairs.' However, Lucinda suspected, no, she knew—the black eye her mother sported had come from her father's fist. Why did she put up with such cruelty? Why couldn't she see she needed to tell someone! Yet trying to get her to admit she needed help was a hopeless task.

The next week dragged on forever. Her father seemed to be somewhat calmer and Lucinda began to relax a little. Perhaps her mother had been right after all; perhaps he would calm down, although she'd experienced the lull between his storms before and knew in her heart it was unlikely. She really needed to find out what was going on about the crash. She needed to know if her father had been made a suspect and if the police were likely to come and interview him, and she was also desperate to see Danny again!

On Sunday morning, not long after her father and mother had left the house to attend church, the doorbell rang. Lucinda was alone in the house and she quickly ran up the stairs to her bedroom. Her father had told her not to open the door to anyone. She peered nervously around the curtains to see who was calling. Her heart skipped a beat when she saw Danny, dressed in his grey hoodie, standing in their porch. She ran down the stairs as quickly as she could manage and shouted desperately through the letterbox.

'Danny, someone will see you, go away!'

'I waited until they'd gone to Church Luce, don't worry. Open the door.'

'I can't, I'm locked in! He always locks me in when he goes out. He says it's to keep me safe in case strangers call. He says it's for my own protection while I'm alone in the house! Please go away Dan, before the neighbours see you and tell him!'

'Ok, don't panic, I just wanted to let you know I've been to the police this morning and told them all I know about the crash. I couldn't ring you in case your father picked up your phone, so I've had to risk coming here. I suspect the police will be arriving soon to question him. I just wanted to warn you, Luce.'

'OK. Thanks. Now please go!' she cried urgently, trying to hold back her tears. 'I'm sorry, I really do want to see you Dan but I'm scared! I'd hate to think what he'd do if he found out you'd been here!'

'OK, don't cry, I'll go now, but I'm going to leave you my phone, Luce, just in case you ever need to get help quickly. Hide it somewhere Luce, somewhere he won't find it! I'll get another one. I'll text you my new number as soon as I get it in case... in case... you need me—and don't hesitate to dial 999 if he turns nasty!'

'Thanks Dan.' He pushed his phone through the letterbox and Lucinda quickly took it and ran back up the stairs to hide it, before peeping out from behind the curtain to see Danny walking briskly away.

It turned out to be a couple of days before the police eventually came to their door, to speak to Brendon about his dangerous driving. They'd looked at the CCTV pictures, but the film had been blurred and hadn't been clear enough evidence to convict anyone. However, once Danny had shown them his video, the pieces all began to lock into place. Now they felt they had all the proof they needed in order to question him.

'What the hell do you mean dangerous driving?' bellowed Brendon, once they were safely inside his house and away from the prying eyes of the neighbours. 'Perhaps you aren't aware of who I am! I think you'd better speak to the vicar, he will vouch for me, and if that's not enough then speak to the headmaster of Linford School.   I'm a respected member of this community! How dare you come into my home and treat me like a common criminal! Now please get out, and make no mistake, I'll be speaking to your Chief Constable, who also happens to be a golfing colleague of mine!'

'We've only come to ask you a few questions Sir, but if you prefer not to answer them here, then perhaps it would be better if we all went down to the station.'

Brendon could see he was cornered. The two policemen standing in front of him were not going to be so easily put off. He knew if he were put into a police car and taken down to the station the neighbours would see him, and he wasn't prepared to endure the shame of that! On the other hand, if the police car continued to park outside his house he could explain to the neighbours he was merely 'helping the police with their enquiries on a community matter', and that would only endorse what a public-spirited person he was. So, he reluctantly opted to be questioned in his home.

Glowering at Maggie as he passed her, he herded them down the hallway and into his lounge where he closed the door firmly behind him. No one was going to listen to this conversation, except him!

'We've had some evidence placed before us Sir, from the CCTV footage taken outside Linford School. We also have a statement, given by a pedestrian, that on the morning of the sixth of September you were driving a red Volkswagen Polo without due care and attention, thereby causing a major road traffic accident. The registration number of that vehicle matches the car parked on your drive.'

'And just who was the person that gave you this information Constable?'

'We're not at liberty to say Sir—but as I've already informed you, we also have CCTV footage.'

'It's taken a while for you to contact me Sergeant. Why is that?'

'Yes Sir, it has indeed. However, it was important, before we contacted you Sir, to make sure the facts we

135

had in our possession were correct. We would not wish to prosecute anyone on false evidence Sir. We've come here today to inform you we will need to interview you tomorrow morning Sir, down at the station.'

'And if I refuse?'

'That wouldn't be sensible Sir.'

Grinning outside, but feeling like thunder inside, Brendon walked the policemen to their car, where he lifted his hand as if to wave them farewell. He was still determined the neighbours, who he knew were hiding behind their curtains, would see nothing, other than him being his usual helpful self, and they would, therefore, deduce the police visit had been linked to his work with the Neighbourhood Watch.

He walked back into his house, anger rising inside him. Once he'd closed the front door all the emotions he'd been keeping in check during the police visit, finally poured out of him like a burst dam. He stormed about the room unable to control himself. He shouted and swore, leaving Maggie and Lucinda cowering in the corner.

'Just look at the two of you! You worthless individuals! Why did I allow my life to be blighted by two useless, pitiful, wretched women like you? Stand up, do you hear me woman! Don't just sit there shaking, you pathetic specimen! STAND UP!'

Maggie slowly got to her feet, and as she did so, she felt the first blow, as the back of his hand made contact with her face and sent her stumbling across the room.

'Leave her alone Dad, It's not her fault!' shouted Lucinda, trying to come between them.

'Not her fault.   Not her fault,' he sang back as he mimicked her voice.

'Whose fault do you think it is then?   Mine?' He pointed at Maggie, 'I've had to put up with her whining and bleating for over twenty years!' He then turned on Lucinda and took a threatening step towards her.   'And you—you're getting more like her every day!   No backbone either of you, simpering, snivelling creatures that you are.   Whatever I did to deserve two miserable wretches like you I'll never know!   Now get to your room girl—NOW!' He screamed the final word, his face now puce with rage.

'No!   I'm not going to leave this room, so you can use Mum as a punch bag as an outlet for your vile temper!'

Brendon stopped in his tracks.   She had answered him back!   How dare she?   He slowly turned around to face her, a look of pure evil in his eyes.   Slowly he walked towards her as she stood her ground.   How dare she, she was provoking him, daring him!   Right, if that was how she wanted it!   He slowly moved towards her.

'You're asking for it girl... asking for it... and by god you're going to get it!'

He raised his hand and hit her across her head, sending her sprawling onto the settee. Still he kept coming, slowly, oh so slowly, and then whack, another backhand slap to the other side of her head. He was now totally out of control, murder blazing in his eyes.

'GET UP!' he screamed, 'Get up and take what's coming to you, you dirty little trollop! Get up you filthy little whore!'

Lucinda was now terrified, she'd never seen him as bad as this and she feared for her life!

'Leave her alone Brendon, leave her alone!' yelled Maggie who was trying to hold his arm to stop him. He elbowed her in the stomach, throwing her off him, his strength seeming immense.

'You gave birth to this ungrateful little tart!' he shouted as he pushed her off. 'You couldn't even get that right! I hope you're proud of yourself woman—but its time she was taught a lesson—get up tart, get up, get up, GET UP!'

Now drooling from the mouth, he began to drag Lucinda up by her hair. She put her hands to her head, crying out in pain as he dragged her to her feet and across the room. She could barely see out of her swollen eyes. He was going to kill her—she knew at that moment he was going to kill her. He threw her onto the settee and launched himself on top of her. She was now choking and gasping for air as she felt his hands tightening around her throat. She tried to claw at his eyes, but lack of air was making her weak and dizzy, so all she could do was to writhe helplessly in panic under him. Suddenly she heard a crack, and through the mist, she saw her mother, with the poker raised high above her head, and she watched in horror as she brought it down upon his head again and again and again!

Brendon's eyes flared in surprise, as he turned to see who had caused his pain. His mouth dropped open to say something and for a moment he looked really hurt that she, his wife, had done this to him. He reached out to her, as if to claim the weapon still in her hand. He staggered two steps towards her—then she hit him again—and slowly, as if in slow motion, he gradually collapsed onto the floor, blood spurting from the open wound in his scalp, covering his hair in a thick, black, sticky, treacly liquid. He laid quite still, on his back, his lifeless eyes staring up at them.

Maggie stood paralysed, staring down at him, confused and seemingly uncertain as to what had caused this. Lucinda slowly rose from the settee and, stepping over Brendon, moved across to her mother. She took the poker gently from her hand and whispered, 'It's all over Mum. He can't hurt us anymore.'

'I did it for you!' Maggie said under her breath, as if not really speaking to anyone. She hadn't taken her eyes off Brendon. She seemed puzzled as if she didn't know who he was, or why he was lying on the ground. Lucinda picked up the throw from the settee and covered it over her father. She had to stop his wide-open eyes from looking at her.

'I'll call the police now Mum'.

Maggie just nodded.

Lucinda ran up the stairs to find the phone Danny had given her and she called him before calling the police.

'Danny, can you come? I think Mum has just killed Dad.'

Tess & Daisy
Chapter 23

Each morning Tess found herself waiting to see if the postman would bring a letter, giving her more insight into how Daisy was coping with life in Durham. She couldn't understand why a child she hardly knew had managed to establish such a hold upon her. Each letter revealed a little more of the child's feelings. Tess had been relieved to see her words had gradually become more and more positive. She recognised she was, at last, beginning to come to terms with her grief. Every single letter Tess stored lovingly away in her desk, in the little office of her two bedroomed semi-detached home in Maidenhead—a treasure to be taken out to be read and reread.

'Dear Tess,

Can you believe it. I've been living with my new family for nearly two years now! I still miss my Mum of course, dreadfully, but I'm beginning to feel a little bit happier. School's been going really well for me! As you recommended, I joined an after-school drama club, and my teacher says I've got an 'aptitude' for it! Hahaha! I've also made some very good friends in the drama group. We're rehearsing for an evening of short plays at the moment. The play I'm in is called 'Dream Jobs'—do you know it? It's about some teenage girls who are day-dreaming about what they'd like to do with their lives. We're going to perform the plays to the parents at the end of term! I wish you lived closer Tess, so you could come and see it, but I know Durham's a long way from where you live, and in any case, you'll be working I expect. I hope I won't feel too nervous and forget my lines! I want you to feel proud of me! I'll pretend you're sitting in the front row of the audience, as I know thinking you're there will help to keep me calm and give me confidence. I'll let you know how it goes, and hopefully I'll be able to send you a photo of us all.

Love from Daisy. X'

'Dear Daisy,

I was so pleased to hear your news! I will certainly be sitting in the audience, in spirit! You could never do anything that would not make me feel proud of you Daisy. You're a very special young lady. I'd so love to be there in person but as you guessed I'll be working. We're also involved in our end of term production and I'm madly trying to make costumes and paint scenery! I hope my pupils are as enthusiastic as you and learn their lines! Some of them are very good but others seem to be leaving it a little late! I expect, as usual, it will turn out well in the end!

I'm very pleased to hear you're now making good friends in Durham. Drama has a way of bringing people together. Your 'cast' will become your family for the next few weeks. Enjoy your applause, as I know you'll get loads, and yes, please send me a photograph if you can. I'll be thinking of you every moment my dear.

Much love to you,

From Tess X'

'Dear Tess,

I don't quite know what to do. My cousin Mattie, who is nearly seventeen, has told me in confidence that she's planning to run away with her boyfriend! I don't want to break her trust, as we're getting along so much better now. What should I do Tess? I don't want to tell anyone what she's planning as she'll hate me, but it's such a big step and I think what she's doing is wrong! The boy isn't even very nice and he's a lot older than she is! If I tell my aunt my life will be hell and Mattie will never speak to me again! What do you think I should do Tess?

Love from Daisy X'

'Dear Daisy...'

Over the next few years, Daisy continued to use Tess as her confidant. She became a person she could trust and one she could turn to when no one else was there for her. She felt she could tell Tess everything; her hopes, her fears and her problems, and Tess responded as she would have done to her own daughter—with love.

She learnt about Daisy's friends and the shopping trips they'd been on. She described in detail dresses she had liked and about the movies they had seen. She even told Tess about the boys she worshipped from afar, and if they'd smiled at her! Later she was told of those that had asked her out on a date. Sometimes Tess detected a slight smudge on the page, where Daisy had allowed a teardrop to fall while she'd been writing about her broken heart. They discussed the plays they'd watched, or been a part of, and between them dissected their merits and their downfalls. They grew closer and closer together with every letter, as the bond between them gradually tightened.

Mary
Chapter 24

Mary was surprised just how much she was looking forward to the next visit to see the skinny little man.

'I can deal easily with him!' she thought, 'he's just a puff of hot air!'

It had been a long time since she'd looked forward to something and even the girls in the office had recorded a smile on the *Parsonometer*. However, they couldn't think why she was smiling and were concerned she could be planning some major adjustments to office procedures. Mary definitely wasn't going to tell anyone about her new lifestyle—certainly not them—and no one would notice anything until she'd gone down at least two dress sizes!

When her Wednesday appointment finally came, she noted the whiter than white teeth in evidence once more, as she entered his interview room.

'I tried to buy black Lycra, but they hadn't got any in my size,' she announced from the door, to cover her embarrassment.

'Then we'd better get to work quick smart so you'll be able to buy some,' he returned, while trying to keep a straight face.

Damn him, straight back with the smart answer, hideous little man!

'So what are we going to do tonight then? I hope you make more progress than you did last week,' she snapped back, 'total waste of time!'

He looked at her. 'OK Miss Parsons, where would you like to begin? The wall bars or the rowing machine?'

'Huh!' she grunted.

'I think perhaps we'll just run through the plan I've prepared for you first though, if you have no objections?'

Bugger him!

'First I have your weekly exercise program.'

He took out a sheet of paper from the file on his desk, read it and then looked up at her.

'To begin with you will WALK to your office each day.'

Mary opened her mouth to complain but Frank quickly continued.

'It should only take about twenty minutes—well it will when you get used to it. I've allowed thirty minutes to begin with.'

He looked down at the next thing he had listed.

'When you arrive at your place of work you will take the STAIR'S and not the lift—EVER! And during the morning you will get up from your desk every thirty minutes and walk around your office.'

'Whatever for?' she returned in surprise.

Frank leant towards her, now smiling.

'For exercise Miss Parsons, in order for you to, exercise! You may even like to stop for a little chat with your colleagues as you pass them by. I'm sure that they'll be surprised and delighted to see you emerge from your inner sanctum!'

'Huh!' she grunted once more.

'And in the afternoon you will do the same again. I need hardly add that at lunch time you will NOT be allowed to eat sandwiches at your desk; I will advise you on healthier lunches. I note there is a park just around the corner from your office, where you will be able to go to eat your lunch and to get some fresh air.'

'And if it's raining?'

'Then perhaps you could sit in the bus shelter, or even frequent the little café around the corner. They serve excellent salads I am told.'

'Huh!'

'You will then 'walk' home from work. I'm not asking a lot from you at this stage Miss Parsons, but if you're not prepared to try what I'm asking, then I'm sure you will agree there would be little purpose in continuing with our sessions,' he smiled again, 'would there? OK?'

They held eye-contact as he waited in silence for her reply. Mary at last managed a reluctant 'Right,' spoken through clenched teeth, her eyes narrowing and hatred seeping from every pore.

'Now let's talk food. I've put together some recipes for you. I've not been extreme; we need to get you into a regime before I apply more drastic measures. Let's see how you get on with these first.'

He passed across a recipe sheet, which she glanced at quickly before pushing aside.

'Of course, there'll be no snacking between meals apart from the suggestions I've given fruit, vegetable sticks and suchlike. Please don't try to cheat as I WILL be able to tell. Now we must weigh you to see if and when your weight begins to come down.'

This was the part Mary had been dreading most of all. She'd never admitted to anyone, least of all herself, just how heavy she was. In fact, it had been so long since she'd been on a weighing machine she didn't even know the answer to that herself!

'Would you rather do this for yourself and fill in this card, or shall I get one of the girls to help you?'

'I'm sure I'm quite capable of weighing myself Sir. I don't need anyone to hold my hand thank you', came her rather too aggressive reply.

He knew that would be her answer—but he'd needed to offer her an alternative in order to make her do it. He realised from experience how sensitive this area would be and rightly suspected she hadn't weighed herself for some time. This could come as a rather nasty shock to her.

And it was! She filled in the card and slammed it face down defiantly upon his desk. He didn't look at it— this had been hard enough for her without the humiliation of someone else knowing. Well, at least that was one hurdle passed.

'I think that's enough for you to be going on with Miss Parsons. We'll discuss other ways of getting exercise on your next visit, things like bowls clubs, dog walking, swimming, cycling—that sort of thing. Think about it and if anything inspires you, or you have any other ideas, let me know.'

He handed her the menus he'd prepared, and she reluctantly took them, knowing full well there was little point in refusing. The little man had made it very clear she had to toe the line if she wished to be kept on the fitness programme.

'Right Miss Parsons, I look forward to seeing you again next week, and maybe by then our plan might have started to work—we will see.'

'Huh!'

'Goodnight Miss Parsons,' he said cheerfully.

All week she tried hard to keep to his plan. She walked to work and quite enjoyed the process. She found she could look in neighbour's gardens and see what they were growing and people would nod to her as she walked past. She gradually got to recognise familiar faces on her route and the nods became 'good mornings'. Of course, it was now summer, if she would feel quite so disposed to it in the winter, with rain and howling gales, she wasn't quite so sure.

Walking up the stairs to her office instead of taking the lift she found to be not so pleasing. By the time she'd arrived at the building she was tired and the staircase stretching before her became her Everest. She held onto the bannister in order to drag herself up each daunting step, annoyed as the fitness freaks ran energetically past, taking two steps at a time. Once at the top, breathing heavily, she shuffled her way across the landing and with tremendous relief entered her office, where she eased herself, exhausted, into her chair.

The first time she did her half hourly wanders around the general office took the office girls totally by surprise! They were amazed to see her wander into their department and their terrified eyes looked at one another, wondering whose name she was going to call out and drag over the coals. To see her do the same thing again half an hour later, and then at half hourly intervals throughout the day, they saw as some new threat to catch them out chatting, or even worse, painting their nails! Was there to be no escape from her darting eyes ever again?

Mary found she rather enjoyed her lunchtime walk to the park, although chatting to people who were determined to share her bench was not so pleasant. By the end of the day, after another thirty-minute walk home, all she wanted to do was to slouch in her armchair in front of the tele, with her take away food tray on her lap. However, that wasn't possible, as the nasty little man had told her she must 'cook' her evening meal—or what he'd referred to as an evening meal on her 'fitness plan'. The few vegetables she was allowed, along with a very small piece of chicken, wasn't enough to keep a fly alive—although perhaps it would be enough for a very small man with whiter than white teeth! How she missed her fish and chip supper, followed by a large gooey lardy cake!

The fruit and vegetable sticks did little to quell her hunger pains and at three in the morning she needed to get up to make a huge mug of low-calorie hot chocolate, in order to get any sleep at all. However, apart from that, she stuck to the plan as if her life depended on it, which, of course it did.

The following Wednesday when Mary, on time as usual, turned up to keep her midweek appointment with Frank, she knew it was to be weigh-in day again and was both nervous and excited to see how much weight she'd lost—or not as the case might be.

He was waiting for her when she emerged from the weigh-in room. She'd lost six pounds—SIX pounds in ONE week! She was so delighted—and smug! She'd already planned what she'd say to him when he covered her with praise and congratulated her for her excellent achievement.

'I'll put him in his place and tell him not to be so patronising!' she thought.

What she hadn't accounted for was that Frank had very quickly summed her up.

'If I praise her she could give in. She likes the challenge, and so a challenge is exactly what I'm going to give her!'

'I've lost six pounds!' she announced proudly.

'Oh dear, is that all!' frowned Frank, 'I think I may need to up the amount of exercise I've given you and reduce the amount of calories. I'll rethink your plan for next week. Never mind, it always takes a few weeks to get everything exactly right. It's my fault as much as yours.'

Mary was furious! She seethed inside! How dare he? She'd never lost six pounds in a week before! She'd never lost six pounds in her life! What the hell did he expect from her! Well she'd show him and if he thought that she was going to give in then he had another think coming!

'I think we should go round the supermarket tonight and get your shopping for the next week. I want to see what you're buying and why your weight is coming off so slowly.'

She looked at him with loathing. She had tried—she had tried very hard! How she hated this silly little man!

The walk around the supermarket was horrendous. She'd never felt so patronised, so humiliated, as she did that evening and there was nothing she could do about it! It was like being a child once again. Whatever she wanted she wasn't allowed to have. He made her read the content of each tin or packet to read it not only silently but also out loud to him! She had to look at the calorie count and the fat content and how much sugar everything contained, and whatever she dared pick up, she had to explain to him why she shouldn't buy it!

After the shopping trip they walked back to her house together, as he wanted to see inside her cupboards. He made her throw away anything that wasn't on his eating plan—on his HEALTHY eating plan!

'How dare he come into my home and treat me like this,' she thought.

But she knew if she said anything he'd drop her like a ton of bricks and she wanted this so much—needed it so much it hurt!

And so, the weeks went by. One evening he even dared to call round uninvited. He wanted to catch her out, to see if she was hoarding food, or even worse hiding it! The packet of KitKats she'd concealed at the back of her cupboard, a little treat for the weekend, was brought out, dangling between his fingers and held out in front of him as if it was the deadliest cocaine and she was a drug dealer. The expression on his face showed nothing but contempt. He told her she was deceitful and if it should ever happen again he would have to speak to his NHS counterparts.

However, week by week her weight came down and secretly they were both delighted. It wasn't long before her slimmer figure became evident to her work colleagues, although no one ever had the courage to voice their thoughts aloud to her. She'd become a regular visitor into their little room and slowly she began to chat to them, and they began to relax and to chat back about things other than work. They'd compliment her on her new clothes, which they noticed were not as frumpy as her old oversized garments. She began to bring in a little colour, a scarf about her neck, and to use lipstick! However, the thing they noticed most was she had begun to smile, and on one occasion even emit a laugh—which was, of course, recorded on the *Parsonometer*!

Gradually Mary found she needed Frank's advice less and less. She'd been his star pupil and he was very proud of her. It was obvious to everyone she was a changed person. She'd even been forced to cancel a few meetings with him because of other commitments. His idea of joining a bowls club had not only appealed to her but she'd found she was also very good at it. She played regularly for the club team, enjoying both the competition and the social aspects of the game. She was excited when they'd begun to rise up the league table, due, she was told, in no small amount to her excellent form!

At one of their Wednesday evening sessions, two years on from their first meeting, Frank suggested it was time for her to go her own way.

'I've taught you all I can Mary, and it's time for me to cut the apron strings. I'm extremely proud how far you've come, and I can see no reason why you should regress.'

They laughed about their initial impressions of each other. They'd become close friends and knew that would never change.

'But don't be surprised if I call in to check your cupboards occasionally, will you?' he laughed.

'Nasty little man', she replied.

'I do have a small gift for you before you go.'

Frank fumbled in his desk draw and drew out a little package, wrapped in gold foil and tied with a red bow. Mary frowned, what was the skinny little man up to now? She looked suspiciously at him before opening the package. Nestling inside she found a packet of KitKats and they both laughed again, as the memory of him finding her hidden hoard came back to them.

'Before you go I do have a little proposition for you Mary.'

Mary waited, unsure what he was about to propose.

'I wondered if you'd be interested, should you have any spare time between work and your bowls matches, to help us out here, at the gym, occasionally? There'd be nothing more motivational for our patients than speaking to someone who's been through the process and has come out the other end. What do you say? Could you spare us some time to give the odd talks? Although I'd rather you didn't tell anyone about my methods. I do need to keep a few things up my sleeve! You never know I may be faced with a cantankerous, overweight, middle aged woman sometime!'

Alan
Chapter 25

Alan watched from behind the curtains of his bedroom window as the Carers drove away. He stared after them until they'd disappeared from view. A feeling of loss suddenly took hold of him. He felt empty. He'd suffered a great deal of pain after the accident—but the pain was better than hollow emptiness. He felt now as if his inside had been dragged from him leaving a vacuum that couldn't be filled. This was real pain. Loneliness was real pain.

He moved pointlessly from room to room, looking for something, anything, to fill the ear-splitting silence. Not finding it upstairs he manoeuvred himself down towards his living room, where he sank into the armchair in front of the television. He closed his eyes feeling the hopelessness begin to engulf him as it seeped further and further into his lonely heart.

He'd had to show his Occupational Therapist he could cope alone before they'd allow him to leave the hospital. They'd put him through a series of tests to prove he could get ready for bed unaided, wash and shave, make a cup of tea and perform any act they considered difficult while his hands were restricted by using crutches. He'd become adept at attaching, walking and removing his prosthetic limb and had passed all the tests given him with flying colours.

'We're confident,' they said, 'that you'll be able to look after yourself very well. We'll be popping back for a few weeks, but I doubt you'll be needing us for long.'

Yet what they hadn't tested—what was impossible to test—was how he'd cope with loneliness. Living alone was so different from the life he'd experienced inside hospital, which was busy and bustling and filled with chatter and laughter. He'd been given help and understanding. While he'd been recovering they'd even given him jobs to do around the hospital to build his confidence, so when he came home he'd be able to do them with ease—and he could—but what they hadn't given him was exposure to silence.

'Stop this,' he thought, 'you can do it, get on with it! Stop feeling so sorry for yourself. The Carers will be coming back soon!'

And they did! However, after a few weeks, when they felt they'd done all they could for him, their visits, the companionship he'd come to rely upon and look forward to, finally stopped. Physically they were right; he was now skilled at getting about his home and doing things for himself. He didn't need them, not for physical things anyway. Nevertheless, now completely alone he mentally retreated further and further into the black hole of his depression.

Initially he'd been pleased his job at Morgan and Taylor had been kept open for him.

'There's no reason you can't continue to run the accounts department like you've always done! After all you're only sitting in an office all day, you'll still be able to do that,' the Head of Department had told him during one of his visits.

At the time he'd been delighted nothing would change. But once home doubts began to creep in. How would he get there? There was no way he'd ever want to catch another bus! He'd never be capable of strap hanging when it was full? He wasn't going to have people feeling sorry for him, and he certainly wasn't going to let anyone see he may sometimes need help! It was easier to hand in his notice, preferring to live on the compensation money he'd been awarded for his injuries.

On rare occasions Health Workers still called. They would fill in their paperwork and report back to the hospital he was doing fine—because that was what he wanted them to believe. He was careful not to reveal how he really felt; his despair. Soon their visits became less and less, until eventually, they came to an end. He didn't need them anymore and he certainly couldn't expect them to go on forever. They had other patients to deal with.

Now he'd no need to 'put on a brave face', no need to wash and shave, no need to cover up his hopelessness. If he did happen to see anyone, the postman or the milkman, he'd lie about his feelings and

159

gradually he began to get sucked deeper and deeper into a hellhole of wretchedness and despair.

The only time he'd make an effort was when he was called to attend a hospital appointment for a check-up. Somehow, he managed to put on a brave face for that, particularly when he popped in to see Nurse Jones. On the surface, everyone thought he'd made a remarkable recovery. However, they didn't see him slouched in his armchair, sitting in his own filth.

Soon he began to cancel appointments saying he was 'too busy'. He'd go for days without washing or eating; what was the point? He didn't need to go out. He got what food he needed from the remains of his once well-stocked freezer or left by the milkman, and when the freezer began to run dry he'd hardly eat anything at all; but he didn't care. His home, the home he'd always kept spick and span, was now grimy, with half-empty cups of tea, their content green with mould, lying around in every room. His kitchen was a battlefield. Dirty dishes were piled high in the sink, and plates of half-eaten food covered the work surfaces. The interest he'd once taken in playing Bridge was long gone and open books and newspapers no longer read, littered the floor, as he slouched in his armchair, unwashed and unshaven, not caring a toss about the havoc that had built up around him.

He'd even stopped answering his telephone, although when he had bothered to answer it in the early days, when so-called friends from work had rung to enquire after his health, he'd always lied and told them he was 'extremely well but very busy at the moment', and it wasn't long before they got the message and stopped calling.

He did make one last extreme effort though—one last visit to see Nurse Jones to thank her for her kindness. On that occasion he made sure he'd shaved and looked clean and tidy. She noticed, with some concern, that he'd lost weight and after he'd gone she'd requested a home visit to check he was eating well. That was when they found the milk bottles on his doorstep!

It had been over a week before his body was found—just as he'd planned. He'd been told health visitors were due to call and knew when they came they'd be anxious to see milk bottles building up on his doorstep. Just as he'd planned each move at the Bridge table, so he'd planned his own final hand—his death.

Alan had always lived his life detached from people. He thought he preferred it that way, until he was involved in the crash, when he'd been forced to communicate. Those that heard of his death presumed he'd found it difficult dealing with the loss of a leg; but that was far from the truth. He'd had no problem coming to terms with that. In fact the accident had given Alan a new zest for living. His weeks in the hospital were the happiest weeks of his life. He'd made friends and chatted to people in a way he'd never done before. It had opened up a new world to him—and when he returned home and found himself going back to his old ways, he realised he didn't want to go along that pathway any more.

So, after he'd taken the tablets and sat in his armchair waiting for the clouds to finally swallow him, he wasn't sad or depressed, because he played over again in his mind the good times he'd had in hospital—and his spirits rose!

As the darkness finally took him he saw the face of the young girl whose head he'd bandaged—and he remembered her beautiful smile—and they sang very softly together :-

'The wheels on the bus go round and round... round and round... round and round.

Wheels on the bus... round and round... all day long.

Bell on the... ding dong... ding... ding...

ding...

Nurse Joyce Jones
Chapter 26

He turned up at the hospital looking fine, a bit thinner perhaps, but he said he'd been advised to lose a bit of weight to help with his walking. I suppose I must have been a bit concerned because I asked for a health visitor to call, just to check he was looking after himself. But apart from weight loss I hadn't seen any real cause to worry. He seemed happy. He chatted as usual. He said he'd just popped in to say hello and the next we heard was he'd taken his own life. Apparently he'd been found by the health visitor when she'd called. It was thought he'd been dead for several days. The poor man had given up. He'd written me a note, apologising, saying he just couldn't cope with his new life:

"Experiencing company, friends and fun in hospital, even without a leg, was better than the loneliness I'm experiencing here in the silence of my own home. I thank you all for your love and your laughter and I hope you will forgive me!"

It isn't him that should be asking for forgiveness, it is me!

It hadn't been the amputation that had led him to taking his own life! Outside the hospital he'd had none of the companionship that he'd grown to enjoy so much while he was with us, and we'd let him down because we hadn't recognised that—we'd failed to look below the surface.

He was so lovely! The last time I saw him I thought he was fine, and we were joking. I'd tried to do what I could for him while he was my patient, but it hadn't been enough!

Why do I do this job? Every day someone dies! I see their heartbroken families gathered around their bedsides. I get to know them, and I'm closer to their loved ones for a time than they are! I wash them, feed them, shave them, take them to the lav. I know them more intimately than I know my own family! Yet when they die no one sees my grief and no one feels my pain.

When their loved ones pass away, I'm the one to reassure them. I let them cry on my shoulder. I collect together all their precious belongings; books, shaving equipment, pyjamas, and sweets! All no longer wanted, all totally meaningless.

What is it all about? What is life all about? The worries, the happiness, work, the act of being, all suddenly stripped away, soon to be forgotten until the next patient comes along to fill the empty bed—and I have to go through all the same crap again! Reassure them—give them hope—wash them—give them some dignity—WHY!

When I began nursing, I wanted to help people, help to make them better, care for them until they were well enough to go home again.   All the nurses and doctors I work with are good people; we do our best! We work long hours to try and keep on top of everything! So why is it all I see is death and sadness, and those that I should have helped take their own life!

I'll leave here tonight and smile as I wave to the night staff, and I'll go home to my family and my husband will say:

'Did you have a good day dear?' and I'll say 'Yes, fine thanks!'

WELL, NO! NO! IT WAS A SHIT DAY! ONE OF MY PATIENTS DIED! HE'D BEEN WITH US FOR A LONG TIME AND WE LET HIM GO HOME BEFORE HE WAS READY! AND I DIDN'T DO A THING ABOUT IT! HE TOOK HIS OWN LIFE BECAUSE WE DIDN'T HELP HIM!

And there's nothing I can do.   I can't even mourn—because tomorrow I'll be doing the same thing again.

And so all I'll say to my husband is, 'Yes it was fine thanks. What would you like for your tea?'

Val
Chapter 27

Recovery for Val was slow and painful, but it was nothing more than she felt she deserved. Being unfaithful had put her in the predicament she was in now. It was her own fault. If she'd been faithful, she wouldn't have been driving along the road at the time of the accident! She felt it was a judgement upon her.

Ben continued to be the perfect husband, looking after her every need. He waited upon her, hand and foot, in the hope that one day she'd own up and tell him the truth. Whatever she was keeping from him, he felt sure he'd be able to forgive. Their love was strong, what could possibly destroy it? Yet deep down he knew things had changed. Trust was missing.

Weeks went by, and still he waited. The second anniversary of the accident went past, and still nothing had been said, and at last, he realised his waiting was to be fruitless.

Val had told him sitting behind a computer desk all day had become too painful, which was true. What she'd omitted to tell him was she neither wanted to tolerate watching Patrick flirting with the office girls— watching some other poor soul being taken in by his promise of adventure. She hoped, by staying at home and becoming a full-time housewife, that one day she and Ben would get back on track—to become again the loving and relaxed couple they'd been before the accident. Whether she was cooking his favourite food or wearing a dress he particularly liked, she did it to show him how dreadfully sorry she was and hopefully to communicate it would never happen again!

However, Ben didn't need her to 'show' him anything, he needed her to 'tell' him! With the words unsaid and smouldering between them, their life became one of constant tension—tension caused by her trying to make things right, trying to overpower him with her guilt, and him going over the top to show her he'd forgive her anything. But while the problem remained unspoken between them neither was getting any real satisfaction from the other.

To the uninformed observer, everything looked wonderful. Two happy people who idolised each other— yet deep down dishonesty and betrayal festered and what had once been love, became pity and what was once warmth, became guilt. It was such a slow process, as slow as Val's recovery, but once they'd passed the two-year anniversary, everything began to change.

She didn't need him to help her quite so much and rather than live the lie each day he chose to work away more often. Val noticed but said nothing. What right had she to judge him? Her days were long, and her nights were lonely. She spent the evenings half-heartedly reading magazines or watching television. She felt alone and unloved and realised she couldn't allow it to go on this way any longer. Whatever had happened to her marriage she had caused—and so she must be the one to try to put it right!

During one long and despondent evening, she sat and mulled over what had gone wrong.

'Why has it gone wrong? Am I solely responsible? Or had it gone wrong long before my affair?'

Val realised in order to save her marriage they would need help. It had been over two years since the accident.

'If we haven't been able to sort it out during that time, then perhaps we need to ask for outside help,' she mused.

The following morning, she plucked up courage and rang a marriage guidance counsellor.

When Ben arrived home late that night, he was surprised to see the light still on in the living room. There was a letter propped up against a vase of flowers upon the coffee table.

***

"Dear Ben,

Things haven't been right between us for some long time and I think you must appreciate that as much as I do. It frightens me to think our marriage is falling apart and that I'm reduced to writing letters to my husband when I want to discuss a matter of such importance. I feel what we once had was too good to allow to disintegrate, without at least putting up some sort of fight in an attempt to try to save it.

I've booked an appointment with a marriage guidance councillor for next Wednesday morning at 10am. I hope you'll try to be there. The address is 29 Randle Terrace. Please come. Love Val''

***

She'd not seen Ben since she'd written the letter. He'd been away again, and she'd seen or heard nothing from him. Neither had he returned home by the time she'd left the house in order to attend the Wednesday morning appointment. She sat, unhappy and apprehensive, in the small reception area, where she hoped upon hope she would see his face appear around the door each time it opened. When 10 am came, and the receptionist called her name, there was still no sign of him, and Val was forced to go into the room alone.

She thanked the Councillor for seeing her, gave her name and address and apologised for Ben's absence. Then it all came tumbling out; why she was there, the accident, and their failing marriage. She was halfway through her ramblings when he appeared, standing in the doorway, apologising for his lateness and explaining his flight had been delayed.

'Your wife tells me she feels you've become distant since her accident Ben; can you explain why that is? I'm not here to judge you, just to get you both to talk.

Marriages so often fail because of a lack of communication.'

Ben was silent for a while, wrestling with his feelings while staring at the wall and watching the second hand of the clock tick by. At last, he cleared his throat and broke his silence.

'I believe my wife hasn't been totally honest with me,' he said simply.

'Is that true Val? Is there anything you'd like to say in reply to this?'

Val took a deep breath.

'I was hoping I need never say these words out loud—but perhaps I was wrong.'

She turned towards at Ben.

'Maybe, to save our marriage, what we both know but have remained silent about for two years, must finally come out. I know your withdrawal and your coldness has been caused by my actions, but I'd thought voicing it would only make it worse!'

Then out it all poured. Patrick, her need for excitement, her fear of losing Ben, her guilt, her loneliness, her reluctance to have children. Things she'd bundled up and hidden inside for so long, and as she spoke an enormous feeling of relief came over her.

Ben listened without looking at her. He showed no emotion upon his face until she'd finished when he closed his eyes and slowly began to shake his head, as if by doing so he could shake out all the things he had just heard.

'All I ever wanted was for you to confess Val, but you didn't, and it's been gnawing away inside me for two whole years! I could have forgiven you back then, I wanted to forgive you. I would have realised how sorry you were and that you really loved me. THAT'S ALL I EVER WANTED TO HEAR VAL! But to live with a lie hanging over us for so long—it became too much!'

Tears were now trickling down his cheeks and Val just wanted to hug him. She wanted to hold him close to her, to tell him how sorry she was and to ask for his forgiveness, but she knew she'd left it far too late for that, and a deafening silence hung in the room as they all tried to take in his words. Then the Councillor spoke.

'I have a feeling that although this may appear to you to be the end of your marriage, it could also be the beginning. You were both very young when you married and you've both made mistakes along the way, as we all do! Ben, you became predictable. While Val was still young and longed for adventure, you wanted her to grow up and to become a mother before she was ready—and she rebelled! Wrong the way she did it, yes, but maybe understandable. You hadn't learned to 'talk', and that is what I suggest you both do for a while. I don't think your marriage is over yet. There is still a chance to save it—if that's what you both really want. It will mean a few lifestyle changes, and it will mean you will both need to be honest with each other, and to TALK! I think you need

171

a little time to process this. So go home and decide if you really want it to end. Come and see me again and we'll take it from there.'

So they talked, and they talked, and they cried, and they cried, until there were no more words and no tears left. Just a new understanding, a coming to terms with what had happened and why it had happened. Slowly their tears turned into smiles and then into laughter, with the realisation that all was not lost.

Tess & Daisy
Chapter 28

"Dear Tess,

I've done it!!!!!!   I've really done it! I've just received a letter from R.A.D.A, and guess what—I've been accepted! Not only have I been accepted, but I've won a scholarship! So I don't have to worry about paying fees! Oh Tess, I am SO excited!

I'll be able to live-in with the other students, which will be great fun! But best of all Tess, I'll be based in LONDON, which means I'll be able to see you all the time! I'll miss my friends in Durham of course, and Mattie! We get along so well now and have become really good 'sisters' at last! Although I bet she'll be over the moon to get her bedroom back to herself once more!

Oh Tess! Isn't it wonderful! You will come and visit me, won't you? And you'll be able to see ALL the productions I'm involved in—PLEASE say you will! I have to rush now as I need to tell all my drama friends, but I wanted you to be the first to know. I love you loads Tess!

Hugs and kisses Daisy. XXXXXXXX'

During the next three years, Tess's life changed dramatically! She and Daisy met up as often as they both possibly could. They explored the shops in the city together, and eat in Covent Garden, where they listened to the many talented musicians performing. They went to theatres, and Tess became a regular visitor at RADA too, where she watched in awe as Daisy developed into a talented and wonderful actress. RADA also discovered Daisy's talent for singing and, it emerged, she'd got hidden dancing skills too, skills which, much to everyone's surprise, she'd grown to enjoy enormously!

For Tess it was no surprise, and she watched with pride as Daisy gradually emerged into a beautiful and outstanding all-round performer. However, she still believed Daisy's real skill still lay in acting. The way she could make her audience laugh one moment and cry the next was spell-binding, and Tess often found she'd become so lost in her performance she totally forgot it was Daisy upon the stage. She had retained her childhood skill and could immerse herself in her character and disappear into an imaginary world, taking her audience along with her.

Instead of going back to Durham during the theatre school's summer vacation, Daisy chose to stay in London and to live with Tess. Mattie had been overjoyed when Daisy had phoned, inviting her to travel up to the big city and to stay with them! How she soaked up the London nightlife! She couldn't believe how vibrant it was in the capital! Durham would always hold her heart, but London was where she envisaged starting her new life!

She couldn't wait to find a job so she could stay there permanently!

Tess had never been so happy, or so busy! With two lively young ladies to keep her on her toes life had never been better! Certainly not since the death of her daughter Ellie had she felt so alive and so needed. Having Daisy around made her feel as if she'd been given a second chance and that she had a daughter back in her life once more.

Maggie Green's trial
Chapter 29

It seemed an eternity to Lucinda before her mother's trial eventually came to court. She'd had to go through the ordeal of her father's funeral first, which, in one of her mother's more lucid moments, she'd begged her to attend. It was the last thing she really wanted, but she couldn't let her mother down. She was so fragile. Lucinda worried that more anxiety would push her over the edge again.

She found the occasion traumatic. Her body was tense, every muscle ridged, as the hearse slowly pulled up at the crematorium. She forced herself to look upon the unadorned coffin and shivered, her heart icy cold. Her mind was telling her, "This is your father; you should feel some love surely," but she felt nothing, nothing but relief, relief to be free of the fear she'd lived with for most of her life. She experienced guilt too, guilt that she felt this way. Surely a daughter ought to mourn her father whatever he'd done—but he'd stolen that emotion, taken that choice away from her!

She sat feeling disconnected during the service and as the curtains slowly drew together, capturing her father's coffin and taking it from her view, she still felt nothing. In the minutes silence that followed, while others in the small congregation reflected upon their own private memories, Lucinda imagined him slowly sliding into the fiery furnace, to be savaged by the angry flames and she felt glad! She was aware of her body relaxing, as all the tension and anxiety of the past few months slowly left her. Only then did she cry, not as most people thought through sadness, Lucinda cried with relief; relief she would never witness him hitting her mother ever again.

Her life seemed to settle down for a while after that. Some days she even forgot what had happened; which made her feel very ashamed. How can you forget your mother killing your father?

Her mother's body had shut down following the dreadful event. She'd been taken into hospital so her mental state could be assessed while she came to terms with what she'd done. Because of Brendon's scheming and devious ways, Maggie had become dependent upon him. In a funny way she still loved him, needed him, and she'd invented ways of forgiving his aggressions. As far as she was concerned, she was guilty of murdering her husband, a good man, who had always looked after her. No matter what anyone said, she went on blaming herself, fully prepared to accept all the punishment she felt was due to her.

It wasn't only Maggie playing the blame game. Geoffrey Stokes too had taken a step back to look at his reflection in the mirror. He'd thought long and hard about what Danny had said to him and, although initially annoyed by his son being so outspoken, had decided he was right. He cast his mind back to look at the reason he'd become a politician in the first place and had come to the conclusion he may well have lost his way. He'd become impregnated with his own importance—not that he allowed his son the satisfaction of knowing that.

'It happened without me noticing Jen,' he confided in his wife. 'I became busy and so full of my own importance that I lost sight of the person I once was. We'd become embedded in our luxurious lifestyle. I'd forgotten the person I'd set out to be all those years ago when we were first married and struggling to get by.'

Jenny laughed. 'They were great days Geoff. Even though we had no money life was good.'

He remembered how she'd supported him during those early days, and how she continued to support him, that was why he loved her and the reason he'd married her. He recalled how happy they'd been, and how, between them, they were going to put right everything that was wrong with the world! They'd done well, and he was, to some extent, very proud of his achievements, but he'd become seduced by the lavish lifestyle and sucked in by his wealthy friends. He'd forgotten the old Geoff and the old Geoff's beliefs.

'It wasn't so long ago that I'd have been the one fighting for justice, just like Dan. I'm ashamed Jen. Ashamed I've allowed myself to put aside my beliefs to become so self-absorbed. I'm even more ashamed it was my teenage son who'd been the first to notice and felt the need to bring it to my attention.'

Geoffrey and Jennifer had talked well into the night, as together they rethought their future. Yes, they still wanted a good lifestyle and they still wanted to send their son to a good school, but there were other things they also wanted—needed—if they were to get back to the people they once were. They'd need to cut their work load, so they'd be home more often. That time would be spent looking after both their constituents and their son.

The following day they told Dan their plan. They also told him they'd agreed to offer Lucinda a home while her mother was being cared for at the hospital.

'She'll need some stability Dan, and she has no one else. We'd like to support her and help you both through the trial, and maybe, should you need it, to offer our advice.'

***

It was the new Geoff who was sitting in the Public Gallery alongside his wife, awaiting the arrival of his son into the witness box, where he'd be providing evidence in the trial of Lucinda's mother, Maggie Green.

TV cameras had camped outside their front door morning, noon and night as the press gathered. A colony of eager ants surrounding juice dripped from an overripe peach, battling for the best position. It had become the story of the week; the right photograph would pay well.

They had the headline already, 'Politician takes murderer's child into his own home' The story of a child whose mother had just been charged with the murder of her husband! However, as so often happens, they soon became bored waiting. Interest was lost when a more newsworthy celebrity offered them a more lucrative option, and they hastily crawled away to follow the trail of a juicier peach.

During the weeks leading up to their court appearance, Danny and Lucinda listened intently as Danny's parents, both well informed on court procedure, advised them what to say and what not to say when they were in the witness box. Danny tried his best to provide Lucinda with all the love, reassurance and protection that he could. He tried to take away her fear, while deep down endeavouring to hide his own feelings, which were equally apprehensive.

'Only answer the questions that you're asked,' advised Danny's father, 'don't go beyond that. It will be difficult, as the prosecution will be looking to catch you out. Keep your answers short and to the point.'

'What about Mum, will she have to go into the witness box too? I don't know if she's strong enough for that yet!' enquired Lucinda.

'There's no need for you to worry about that, her doctors will decide if she's well enough. You must only focus upon yourself. There'll be plenty of time for you to support your mum when it's all over. She'll be given lots of advice and a lot of help from her lawyer. They've given her bail so that's a good sign. No doubt she'll be advised to plead guilty to manslaughter.'

It was almost a relief when the day of the trial finally arrived. At least now they could stop thinking about what 'might' happen and concentrate on what 'was' happening!

As Lucinda battled through the reporters camped outside the Old Bailey, their camera's flashing in her face, temporally blinding her, she felt terrified. She recognised other familiar faces around her as she walked inside— people who'd also been called to give evidence. She saw her Head Master and the Reverend Graham, but they purposely turned their heads away as she passed. She was then taken into an ante-room, where a lawyer took her over her statement.

Inside the courtroom Maggie Green was brought into the dock, looking ashen-faced and hollow-eyed, as if she'd not slept for weeks, which was in fact very true. She glanced up to the public gallery with unseeing eyes.

Jennifer Stokes sat looking down and could feel nothing but sympathy. The poor woman looked so confused and frightened. Her only crime had been to protect her daughter; surely every mother on the jury would recognise that. She noticed Maggie's eyes quickly scan the jury before lowering her head and casting her eyes straight down into her lap.

Council for the Prosecution, a tall, thin man with rimless spectacles, wearing his official courtroom robe and silver wig, rose to his feet and looked around the court before addressing the jury.

'It is my duty to put before you today, the facts, and it is your duty to decipher those facts. After listening to the witnesses I put before you, it will be YOU who will determine if Margaret Jane Green is guilty of murdering her husband, Brendon Reginald Green, or not.'

He paused as he looked at the jury before continuing.

'It will be YOU who will decide if it was done in self-defence, or in the defence of her daughter Lucinda Rose Green—OR—did she in fact 'lose control'? Was the attack on her husband out of proportion and designed, not only to render him harmless—but indeed to kill him?'

He paused once more to allow the jury to take in his words.

'It is YOU, Members of the Jury who will decide if Margaret Green used reasonable force to protect herself and her child, or did she—in a moment of extreme anger 'intend' to kill him?'

He now cleared his throat.

'I will be calling upon witnesses to give evidence to prove that the defendant and her husband were heard arguing on several occasions and that their relationship was not an entirely happy one. It will be left to you to decide if this was indeed manslaughter or—was it wilful murder?'

After casting his eyes over each member of the jury Mr Marcus Reed QC sat down.

Maggie's lawyer then rose from his seat and put before the jury his reasons for thinking Maggie 'acted as any mother would to protect her child'. He pointed out that she hardly looked like a murderer; in fact she had never done harm to another being in all her life.

'I will prove to you that unprovoked aggression is not in any way a part of Maggie Greens character. I will also prove to you, members of the jury, just what a loving wife and mother she is. She is, I believe, incapable of wilful murder and if, after hearing all the evidence from my learned friend and myself, if you are still in ANY DOUBT that Maggie Green is capable of wilful murder, then you must bring in a verdict of not guilty' He then resumed his seat.

Marcus Reed rose to his feet once more. 'I would like to call my first witness; the Reverend William Graham.

Reverend Graham bustled into the courtroom where he was escorted to the witness box. He took the Testament in his right hand and read the oath with feeling from the card.

'I understand you are the vicar of St. Andrews, the church attended by the late Mr Brendon Green?'

'I am indeed Sir.'

'Could you tell the court what kind of person you found Mr Green to be?'

'He was a good man Sir. He attended church regularly and our parishioners had much to thank him for! He was also a great help to me personally.'

'In what capacity did he help you Reverend?'

'He never missed a sermon and each Sunday he gave up his time to hand out the hymn books and to help me welcome the congregation as they arrived. He was wonderful at organising people into doing all the little jobs that are needed for our church to run so efficiently. He was indeed a great help to me.'

'Would you say he was an aggressive man?'

'Certainly not sir, he was always very happy to help anyone and everyone. He was a respected and much-admired member of our little community!'

'Did you ever have cause to wonder about the relationship he had with his wife?'

'Good gracious, no Sir! I always thought what a devoted couple they were. He couldn't do enough for his family. On the occasions I attended their home for dinner I found him to be most agreeable.'

'Thank you Reverend. No more questions.'

Mr David Lowe, QC, Council for the defence, stood up and paused as he scanned the notes before him. Then, frowning, he looked up.

'Good morning Reverend Graham. You say you had —er—a good relationship with the deceased?'

'I did indeed Sir.'

'And yet I have a note here from one of Mr Green's neighbours, who claims to have overheard you calling Mr Green—and I quote 'an interfering busy-body.' He smiled at the reverend. 'Is that correct?'

'Er…. um…. well…. that may have been true…. Um…. there were times ….' Reverend Graham seemed flustered and stumbled over his words, before continuing quickly 'but on the whole I appreciated his help.'

'Thank you for clearing that up for me Reverend. That will be all.' Mr Lowe sat down, smiling, as a troubled Reverend Graham left the witness box.

Mr Hinton, Lucinda's Head Master, was the next character witness to be quizzed by the prosecution.

'Good morning Mr Hinton. I believe Mr Green played an active role at his daughter's school. Could you tell the jury what he was like as a member of the Parent Teacher Association?'

'Mr Green was a valued member of the PTA, Sir and he was also a personal acquaintance of mine.'

'And his daughter, Lucinda, in your opinion was she a happy child?

'Lucinda is one of my brightest pupils. Her father took a great deal of interest in her education. Yes, I believe she was a very happy child and he was a devoted father.'

'Thank you, Mr Hinton.' Mr Reed sat down as Mr Lowe came to his feet.

'A personal acquaintance?' enquired Mr Lowe.

'Yes, I had the honour to sit around his dinner table on more than one occasion.'

'And the family's relationship with each other on those occasions was …?'

'From what I saw it seemed very good to me Sir. Margaret Green was always busy in the kitchen, she didn't sit at table, it was a 'men only' occasion you see.' Mr Hinton smiled.

'I see. And where was Lucinda Green, his daughter, during those occasions?'

'She was always in her bedroom doing her homework I believe.'

'So his wife and child were kept strictly away from your… um… 'men only' gatherings? Thank you Mr Hinton. That will be all.'

Various neighbours were then called by the prosecution as character witnesses for Brendon, each painting him as an amiable man and a devoted husband and father, a man who was always willing to help anyone that needed it, and sometimes when they didn't, and a tireless Neighbourhood Watch member.

After they'd all finished painting Brendon as whiter than white, the court adjourned for lunch.

After lunch it was the turn of the defence council to call his witnesses.

Danny was the first to be called. His legs were shaking as he stood in the witness box, his mouth dry and his hands sweating and clammy. As he looked nervously up into the public gallery, he was relieved to see his Mum and his Dad (who gave him a slight nod of encouragement) sitting in the front row.

Mr Lowe rose from his seat.

'You are Danny Stokes a school friend of Lucinda Green?'

'Yes Sir.'

'You were a witness to the road traffic collision that happened outside Linford School, and I understand you captured the moment on your mobile phone? Is that correct?'

'Yes Sir.'

'You accompanied Lucinda to the hospital in the ambulance I believe?'

'Yes Sir.'

'Can you tell the court what her father's reaction was when he arrived at the hospital and heard you had accompanied her there?'

'He appeared very angry and told me to go away, Sir.'

The prosecution leapt up offering the opinion that Brendon had been in shock, and it was reasonable to believe he'd only been 'looking out' for his daughter. He had, after all, never met Danny before and knew nothing of him.

Mr Lowe then continued. 'Did Mr Green allow you to see his daughter while she was in hospital,' he glanced across at Council for the Prosecution, before continuing, 'AFTER he'd found out you were a school friend of hers?'

'No Sir he didn't. He didn't allow her to see anyone. She wasn't allowed to have any friends—boys or girls. Lucinda was frightened of her father Sir.'

'Frightened of her father? Surely not! Why was that do you think?'

'She wasn't frightened for herself Sir. She was frightened he'd take it out on her mother if she disobeyed him.'

'Did she tell you the reason for this?'

'She told me she often heard them arguing and that she'd heard her father shouting and cursing her mother, and sometimes she saw bruises on her mother' body.'

The prosecution jumped up again.

'Heard them arguing! So it seems they were not such a devoted couple after all!' He turned and delivered his next words straight at the jury. 'The Green's marriage, it now appears, seems to have had its problems.' He turned back to Danny. 'Are we now to understand Brendon and Margaret Green were not the devoted couple we have been led to believe?'

'No, I didn't mean that!' stammered Danny.

'Please don't try to lead the witness Mr Reed,' interjected the Judge.

'I'm sorry Your Honour. So what did you mean Mr Stokes?'

'I just meant she was frightened her father may lose his temper and hit her mother, so she avoided any conflict and tried not to annoy him.'

Danny's heart was pounding. Had he said the wrong thing? Had he got Lucinda's mother into even more trouble? He hadn't meant to! His father had told him only to answer the question asked—but they have a way of getting you to say things and twisting your words! He felt relieved when he was allowed to stand down—but not before the embarrassment at having to tell the court how he'd captured the accident on his mobile phone, while taking a secret photograph of Lucinda with rain-soaked hair!

Detective Sergeant Wilson, the policeman who had visited the Greens prior to the murder, was the next to be called by Mr Lowe.

'You were sent to the home of Brendon Green on the morning of the...er...' Mr Lowe referred to his file, 'fourteenth of October, could you tell the court how this came about please Sergeant.'

'Certainly, I can Sir.'   Sergeant Wilson took out a little black notebook and thumbed his way through the pages until he came to the one he needed. He then cleared his throat and began speaking in a strong and clear voice in order that no one in the courtroom would miss a word he said.

'On the morning of the fourteenth of October, I attended the home of Mr Brendon Reginald Green, regarding an RTC that had occurred on the sixth of September. We had received evidence that Mr Green had been instrumental in causing that incident and I had been sent to his home to interview him.'   He beamed broadly at the jury.

'Can you tell the court how Mr Green reacted when you spoke to him, Sergeant?'

'At first, when we was on his doorstep, Mr Green appeared happy to talk to us Sir, but once we was inside his home he became very angry and he asked us to leave. I then advised him that if he preferred to answer our questions down at the station he was at liberty to do so, at which point he invited us into his living room.'

The Sergeant then referred to his little book.

'I then explained we'd obtained CCTV footage of the incident and that a pedestrian had also handed in a mobile phone video. The said video had shown Mr Green driving out into the traffic without due care and attention. I informed him this action appeared to be the cause of a major road traffic collision, whereby one woman lost her life and others sustained serious injuries.'

Sergeant Wilson looked up from his little notebook.

'Mr Green was then invited to come down to the station to make a formal statement Sir.'

'He had calmed down a little by that time I presume.'

'He had Sir. By the time he showed us off his premises he appeared very jovial, Sir, smiling and waving us on our way.'

'While you were in his home did you see his wife and child at all?'

'Only very briefly Sir, as Mr Green led us down the hallway and into his front room. He then closed the door firmly behind us Sir.'

'Thank you Sergeant.'

After some cross-examination Sergeant Wilson left the witness box and the Judge suggested it a good place for the court to break for the day.

***

Lucinda tossed and turned all night. When she slept, she dreamt her father was bearing down on her, telling her she'd been responsible for his death. When she was brought into the courtroom the next morning, she looked pale and wan, her eyes terrified. She stood in the witness box looking such a frightened little thing that the Judge felt compelled to speak to her with compassion.

'I realise this is a very frightening experience for you Lucinda. I want you to know you'll be able to stop the questioning at any time if you feel it becoming too much for you. You have lost your father, and your mother is standing in the dock accused of his murder. Thankfully this is not a situation many of us will ever experience in our lives. Unfortunately you will be taken back to that fateful day—but I'm sure my learned friends will try to make the process as painless as they possibly can for you.'

'Thank you,' Lucinda replied her voice a whisper.

The defence lawyer stood up.

'Hello Lucinda. I will try to be brief but there are some questions I do need to ask which may be difficult for you. Please just take your time, there's no rush.' Mr Lowe paused as he looked down at his notes. 'When the police had left your house on the morning of the 14th of October after they'd questioned your father about the accident, how did your father react?'

'He was very angry Sir.' Lucinda remembered the advice Danny's father had given her about keeping her answers short and to the point.

'How did he show that anger Lucinda?'

'He shouted at us, me and Mum. He called us horrible names. He made Mum stand up and he—he hit her!'

Lucinda's hand covered her mouth in an attempt to stop her crying as she remembered the scene. She bit her bottom lip.

'And what did you do, Lucinda?'

'I tried to tell him to stop—I told him it wasn't Mum's fault!'

'And what happened next?'

'He told me to go to my room.'

'And did you?'

'No. I knew if I did he'd hit Mum again—but he didn't like me disobeying him!'

'So, what did he do then?'

'He turned on me! He hit me! Again, and again and again! Mum begged him to stop but he wouldn't! He started to drag me across the room by my hair!' Her hands went up involuntarily to her head, as if once again feeling the pain. 'I'd never seen him look so angry—never seen him like that—he looked like an angry dog—wild and drooling!'

Unable to contain her feelings any longer the words came pouring out as she once again remembered and relived the terrifying scene. 'I knew he was going to kill me! He put his hands around my throat—I couldn't breathe! Mum begged and begged him to stop but he wouldn't—and his grip got tighter and tighter and tighter until I was choking!'

Lucinda was now sobbing as she recalled the last moments of her father's life—the last memory she would ever have of him—the memory that for the past few months she'd been trying to erase from her mind.

'Could someone pass Lucinda some water please? I think perhaps the court should now take a short recess, for about an hour,' suggested the Judge.

Maggie had been listening to her daughter's account, her head in her hands. She was also being made to relive that fateful day. She could see Brendon in front of her, strangling their daughter and she screamed out. 'I'm so sorry Lucinda, I'm so very, very sorry. Please, forgive me!' She began sobbing, saliva dribbling from her mouth and her nose running uncontrollably. Distressed as she tried to reach out to comfort her daughter and now totally out of control she rose waving her arms in the air in an unsuccessful attempt to reach Lucinda. She struggled to fight off the restraining hands that were holding her back. Her only aim was to comfort her beautiful child—to help her shut out the dreadful vision that lay before her—yet all the time being aware it would be one vision that neither of them would ever be able to erase from their memories. She felt the cold metal of the poker once more in her hand, and she brought it down as if in her imagination she was hammering it again and again and again into her husband's head, denting the wooden shelf in front of her!

It was to be well over an hour before the court resumed. Lucinda had somehow managed to recover her composure, and Maggie had been given some sedation and her hand bandaged. She was once again sitting quietly in the dock.

'Is it alright if we continue Lucinda?' Mr Lowe spoke softly. 'Do you feel able to tell the court what happened next?'

Lucinda swallowed and nodded. 'Yes Sir.'

He then spoke slowly and gently. 'Before the judge called for a recess, you were telling us you thought your father was going to kill you, Lucinda. Are you able to tell us what happened next—after your father had put his hands around your neck?'

'Yes.' Lucinda's voice was barely audible as she continued. 'He was strangling me Sir and I couldn't breathe. Then I saw Mum hit him with the poker. She didn't mean to hurt him; she only wanted him to leave me alone!'

'How many times did she hit him Lucinda?'

'I don't know. Three, maybe four, I'm not sure. Dad looked surprised at first and turned his head round to look at her—but Mum hit him again ... until he let me go ... then he fell down onto the floor.'

The prosecution then got to his feet and paused before he said, 'Did your mother hit your father 'after' he had fallen to the ground Lucinda?'

Lucinda looked across at her mother, who gently smiled back at her daughter and gave a slight nod of consent. Lucinda's lips trembled, and tears cascaded down her cheeks as she whispered, 'I think so Sir.'

'Thank you Lucinda.'

Mr Marcus Reed, Council for the Prosecution, sat down, having taken no pleasure from asking the child that question, as he knew her answer would probably be the one that would send her mother to prison.

Tess & Daisy
Chapter 30

Daisy came flying in through the front door shouting, 'I've got it! I've got it! Tess, where are you? I've got it!'

Tess, who'd been in the bathroom washing her hair, came to the top of the stairs with a towel wrapped around her head, wiping her eyes.

'What on earth has happened?'

'I've got it!

'Got what?'

'I've got the part! It's enormous Tess! The lead! No more coming to see me in some little provincial theatre, now it's a front row seat for you—in the West End! I've only gone and got the part of Jane Eyre at the National!'

Tess stood open-mouthed before the two rushed into each other's arms.

'That's wonderful news! Oh Daisy, you deserve it so much! You've worked so hard for this! I'll not be wanting just one front row seat—I'll want the whole front row! I'll want to bring everyone I know to see you on your first night! I'm so proud of you my darling!'

They hugged each other again, neither able to contain the joy they felt inside them.

During the next few weeks Tess was walking on air, and, as promised, bought most of the tickets in the front row of the stalls. She couldn't wait for the first night to arrive. However, after two months of intense rehearsals, it was upon them. She sat in the middle of the front row waiting for the lights to go down, feeling a thousand butterflies fluttering about inside her. She knew the lines almost as well as Daisy, as she'd gone over them with her so many times!

The evening seemed to be over in a flash and when the curtain finally fell at the end of a magical and memorable first night, only to rise again and again and again to shouts of 'Bravo', the audience standing on their feet while they clapped and cheered in appreciation, Tess's felt her heart would burst with pride, and so much love.

Daisy stood centre stage enjoying the moment and as she looked down upon her adopted mother she noticed the tears glistening on her cheeks. She smiled, put her hand on her heart, and blew her a kiss. She knew, without a doubt, that if it hadn't been for the woman sitting in the centre of the front row, this night would never have been possible.

A big party followed to celebrate their successful first night, during which Tess was introduced to a young man called Mark. Daisy explained that he worked backstage, and Tess could see immediately, by the twinkle in their eyes, that this friendship was something very special. She'd been introduced to Daisy's boyfriends before, but she'd never seen Daisy looking at any of them in quite the way she was looking at this young man.

The following morning rave reviews littered all the newspapers, and over the next few months Daisy continued to float on a cloud of happiness, as she soaked up all her plaudits—and fell deeper and deeper in love with Mark.

By the time the play reached its first anniversary Daisy and Mark had announced their engagement and by the time the second anniversary came around, their wedding arrangements were in full swing!

It was a very quiet wedding held in a small hotel near to the theatre. Guests were kept to an absolute minimum, just Daisy and Mark, along with Mark's parents, Tess, and of course Maddie—who had found it so difficult to keep the secret. She was to be 'the star's bridesmaid', and she wanted to shout it from the roof-tops! However, she managed to keep it to herself long enough for the ceremony to take place, but as soon as it was over her phone began overheating as she rang all her friends. It was a beautiful day at the end of September and as the late summer sun cast its golden rays upon Daisy, looking so perfect in a simply cut cream dress with a matching jacket, it was obvious to everyone that the bride and groom only had eyes for each other.

At the tiny reception, held in an upstairs room at the hotel, away from the prying eyes of the media, Daisy stood to give her short speech, which was simple and heartfelt. She thanked everyone for coming—the special people in both their lives. She thanked Mark for falling in love with her, and Maddie for 'eventually' becoming her closest friend and 'the best sister anyone could have!'

Then she turned to Tess, raised her glass, and smiled.

'To Tess, who has been my inspiration. To Tess, who has shown me how to love and who gave me a purpose to live! To Tess, who offered me her support to enable me to realise my dreams. To Tess, who offered me her life!'

With watery-eyes Tess then replied.

'My darling girl, I never gave you anything you haven't paid back to me in full! You say I gave you my life—but my life wouldn't have been worth living without you in it!'

The Aftermath

'It's not what happens to you, but how you react
to it that matters'

Epictetus

Geoff & Jennifer Stokes
Chapter 31

Jennifer Stokes sat curled up on the sofa, her head nestling in her husband's chest. It felt so good. She inhaled deeply, and as she slowly released her breath, she felt more relaxed than she'd done in a very long time.

'This is so good.' She smiled up at her husband. 'I'd forgotten what it was like to just sit and appreciate what we have.' She snuggled back into the curve of his arm. 'I thought we'd got the perfect life, but now I realise life is only perfect if you keep track of the things that really matter. We'd spent so much time working we'd lost sight of each other. Thank goodness we realised before it was too late.'

Geoff kissed the top of his wife's head.

'I guess Lucinda's father had also done that—forgotten to appreciate what he'd got—and to remember how far he'd come.'

'Yes, I suppose he had. You know Geoff there are times when I actually feel quite sorry for him. He had such high ideals. If he hadn't caused that accident he'd most likely still be handing out hymn books in church on Sunday.'

'The trouble was, in Brendon's case,' returned Geoff, 'the accident was only the tip of the iceberg. He was a ticking timebomb waiting to go off and the accident was the thing to ignite him. Unfortunately, the unstable background he'd endured from the day he was born hadn't helped.'

'And yet he'd tried so hard to free himself from his past.' Jennifer frowned and sighed again. 'I suppose it was just too late and it had become part of him. All he'd ever wanted was to be accepted into a middle-class society, and just when he thought he had it firmly in his grasp it was taken away from him again—by just one careless moment.'

They sat in silence for a while until she continued.

'I don't think he ever questioned if it was wrong when he hit Margaret, he'd seen his father do it so many times to his mother. In his mind Margaret deserved it. He thought she needed to be taught respect, needed to know, as his mother had known, that she was... the underdog... and must learn to bow down and worship him. As he saw it, he was her husband, and her role was to glorify his image! I'm not trying to condone what he did; heaven forbid—but to some extent I can understand it.'

'He'd' become confused my love. He'd been taught a lot of bad lessons. He saw Margaret's loyalty as a fault, and hiding her faults from the outside world was just another example of what a tolerant and forgiving man he was. He'd inherited his father's volatile temper, and had probably seen his mother go through some horrendous things when he was a child. He'd been taught it was the right way for a husband to behave. I think controlling his family enabled Brendon to get some relief from the pent-up anger inside him.'

'Lucinda said he was like a sergeant major controlling his troops! Oh Geoff, I do hope she doesn't blame herself. It was so sad the way it turned out. Maybe if Maggie had been stronger and spoken out about his aggressive behaviour, he might have been given the help he needed. Her weakness played into his hands. If she'd stood up to him the whole situation may well have been averted, who knows?'

'He'd tortured her slowly Jen—and for so long she didn't recognise it as cruelty. She saw it as normal loving behaviour, to be forgiven, because he'd convinced her it was always her fault. They were two people whose lives should never have collided.'

'You're right. Maggie was weak; she'd lacked confidence. I bet when she met Brendon she thought herself lucky to have found someone like him. Someone prepared to take all responsibility away from her. I suspect for a long time she even enjoyed it and was happy to allow him to do it. Life must have been easier for her that way. She'd got someone to think for her and to look after her, and I think she probably really loved him!'

'It was sad she hadn't noticed they'd moved on and he'd slowly taken over her mind. She hadn't realised she'd become his plaything, his toy, to manipulate as he wished, until he'd removed every shred of her self-respect.'

'I guess if it hadn't been for the crash Maggie would still be making excuses for him. Oh, Geoff, it's so easy to lose sight of where you're going! We must learn from it. We must never again become greedy and lose sight of our beliefs. Perhaps we do have something to thank them for.'

'We do! We have Lucinda—and she makes our son very happy. Come on now, cheer up! Let's have a night-cap before we turn in. I have constituents to see tomorrow!'

Nurse Jones
Chapter 32

Three miles away Joyce Jones was staring into her hot chocolate. She'd been to bed, but her mind was restless, so she'd come downstairs so as not to wake her husband. She sat at the kitchen table, trying to work out what she should do with her life. Thoughts were tumbling about in her head.

Her husband's face peered around the kitchen door.

'What's the matter old girl? Can't you sleep?' he asked.

'Oh, sorry did I wake you? I tried not to.'

Paul, her husband, was worried. He'd seen a change in his wife over the last few weeks. She'd seemed distracted and, although he'd asked a couple of times if she had a problem, she'd brushed his questions aside.

'Come on, out with it. I can't help if you don't talk to me.'

Joyce got up from her chair and walked across to switch on the kettle.

'It's silly really Paul,' she told him. 'But I just can't get a patient out of my mind. I've been feeling disillusioned for a while now, with the job, but it wasn't until I met Alan that it was brought into sharper focus for me?'

She recalled what he'd told her. She knew he'd never been an exciting person, but he appeared to have vaguely enjoyed his life, in his own solitary way. He'd asked for little, except to be left alone.

'How do you mean? You've always loved being a nurse. What's changed?'

'It was while he was in hospital I suppose I noticed ways we were letting him down. 'He' changed in a good way. When he came in he had little hope, but after a while he had a glimpse into the world he'd been missing. Suddenly he caught sight of what his life could really be like, but although, in his heart, he wanted it more than anything, he knew he'd left it far too long and it was too late. The idea of such a transformation became just too disturbing for him.'

Joyce passed a hot drink to her husband and they sat across from one another at the table. She continued talking while Paul listened.

'He'd been offered the possibility of a new and exciting beginning. A new start had suddenly opened before him and it was one he was eager to explore. For a time, he'd been excited by it and thought it a challenge he'd be able to persue. But once he'd returned home, the idea became totally unrealistic. He knew he was too set in his ways. While he'd been with us in hospital he'd felt safe and thought it attainable, and for a short time he'd become a different person—we all saw that! He was more confident, and I think he thought this new life was within touching distance. But once we'd released him and he'd gone back home, he found nothing had changed, and the new life was just too far out of his reach.'

Paul cut in, 'I don't understand. None of that's your fault,' But Joyce continued talking, staring down at the wood-knot in the table, deep in thought.

'For years he'd been satisfied to put up with his lonely world, not knowing or understanding friendship and comradery, and once he'd experienced it and enjoyed it, he became.... dissatisfied. He didn't want to return to his old life and yet wasn't able to access the new one. Alan's past had become his downfall. He used to chat and tell me about his childhood. He was a product of the person his parents had encouraged him to become... and it was too late for him to change that. His early life was so embedded within him he couldn't see a way out and the whole thing became too frightening for him.'

'Did he have friends—relations?'

'No. Sadly, there had been no one to miss Alan. There were few people to attend his funeral.'

They sat quietly for a moment, sipping their drinks. Joyce then looked up and when she spoke it was with passion.

'Paul, when I'd started nursing I'd been a lively young junior nurse, remember? I was always happy, cheerful and content to look after those around me. Helping people was in my blood and I got an enormous sense of achievement when I saw patients recover enough to go home. You know that all I'd ever wanted was to care for the sick and the vulnerable... and for a time that worked, and I felt fulfilled... that was why I followed my heart and became a senior nurse with responsibility... even though it meant longer hours and lots of studying.'

'Are you saying you want to give up? If you feel like that you know I'll support you.'

Joyce shook her head.

'With responsibility came awareness... and now all I can see are the cracks in the system. I've come to realise I'm unable to care for my patients as diligently as I'd like; as I feel they deserve. And I feel the most enormous amount of guilt! The system is letting my patients down—letting me down—by not allowing the time and the finances for me and my staff to do our jobs as well as we feel they should be done. Overwork, longer hours and lack of funding, being asked to perform tasks that we haven't been trained for. I'm being asked to administer drugs to patients and to make treatment judgements. These are jobs that had once only been undertaken by trained doctors. The wage I receive, although much less than the doctors who'd done it in the past, is irrelevant. As far as I'm concerned this is not about money, it is about the safety of my patients. I'm becoming unable to detach myself from them because I feel they're getting such a raw deal and being so poorly treated. They're being left in corridors for hours until a bed becomes available for them on the ward. They're being sent home far too soon after surgery—and they're not being given the aftercare that I know they need—and deserve.'

Tears filled Joyce's eyes. Paul had never seen her so wound up about her work before. If this was how she felt then she should walk away. They needed the money she was bringing in to pay off the mortgage but that was unimportant compared with her wellbeing. He couldn't bear to see her so distressed.

'The system was partly responsible for Alan's death, Paul,' continued Joyce. 'I know only too well the doctors and nurses are doing all they can. They're all working long hours and are just as dedicated as they've ever been, perhaps more so. I can't help but feel that, as part of the system, I should be doing more for those in my care, and if that isn't within my power then I question if I want to remain in the profession I once loved so much. But, along with those doubts comes the nagging question … if I and my colleagues—who I know have similar feelings, if we left, what would become of our patients? Who would there be to care for them?'

Mary & Frank
Chapter 33

Outside the studio stood a life-sized cut out with the words:

OPENING SOON!

A new studio designed to help and encourage the overweight and the obese, those who feel too shy or self-conscious to go to a normal gym and who need support and motivation to conquer their weight problem.

Allow us to help you! We have personal experience of your problem and are after your lbs not your £'s. Begin your new year with hope!

Contact either Miss Mary Parsons or Mr Frank Fielding.

It had taken a crash to push Mary from the predictable life she'd created, and although traumatic, had sent her staggering towards a diversion in her road, forcing her along a path she'd previously been too scared to venture down. Here she was enticed to explore a new, frightening, and very different pathway. However, having trodden it she could see the possibilities stretching out before her and she'd become excited, and being excited was something Mary didn't do. Excitement wasn't in her nature—not even with fitness freak Frank! Even now, after all the time they've known each other, she still plays her cards close to her ample chest. Mary is, and always has been, a fighter, and she'd been introduced to a man who liked a challenge! Between them they'd made the perfect cocktail.

Eventually they fell in love. Oh! Not a story-book romance type of love, like you find between the pages of a woman's magazine. Oh no! Their love is something far stronger than that. Theirs is a platonic love, embedded deep within them. It's a love certainly more loyal than many marriages will ever be.

Before they'd been thrown together, they were both perfectly content with their lot! They'd lived alone for many years and were pretty set in their ways—and that will certainly never change! Living together would be their downfall!

Ignoring the fact they both needed someone in their life and being too stubborn to admit they were lonely, they'd convinced themselves they were better off on their own. For them it wasn't a sexual relationship that either of them craved. What they needed was plain old-fashioned friendship—a friendship which has become stronger and increasingly more loving and caring over the years—although don't voice that to them, particularly to Mary, or you'll find yourself like the girls in the office, out on your ears.

Mary and Frank don't ask for anything from each other, except perhaps loyalty—although Frank still seethes when arriving home after an evening spent in her living room, discussing patient progress, to find Tabatha's hairs glued to his trouser legs! He grimaces as he remembers the day he foolishly ventured to mention this to her.

'If you find it so distasteful,' she spat out, 'then you needn't bother to come! Tabatha is my best friend and constant companion and if you can't accept that, then perhaps you should stay away! I find Tabatha much nicer than most people—and certainly more loyal!'

Of course, she didn't really mean it, not all of it. Frank is just as important as Tabatha in Mary's eyes, well, almost. They are the two constants in her life and god-help anyone who tries to put either one down! Mary's fighting spirit goes hand in hand with the self-preservation she's built around herself in order to survive; and Frank knows her well enough now to realise he'd be well advised never to mention cat's hairs to her ever again! He has since learnt to curse quietly to himself whenever he finds one of the 'disgusting intruders' embedded annoyingly into his clothes!

For the most part, Mary and Frank make each other smile—they understand each other so well! Their relationship will last forever, never sexual, just loving, being there for each other, supporting each other, working alongside each other; and sometimes, heaven forbid, even 'listening' to each other!

The crash had inadvertently set Mary on a path to find someone who would understand her and give her the strength and motivation to change her life. She has at last come to terms with the father that abused her and took away her childhood. Frank taught her how to find self-respect and gain personal satisfaction by helping others. Had it not been for the crash she'd never have been given that opportunity.

Of course, she'll never be a perfect size eight, and her big-boned five-foot ten-inch frame still towers over five-foot six-inch Frank, but the pounds continue to come off, and she now weighs in at a respectable twelve stones—and life feels good!

It was five years after their first meeting when they opened their studio. A cut-out of Mary, as she'd been when Frank first met her greeted everyone as they entered, along with a speech bubble saying the words, 'If I can do it, so can you!'

Calls to the telephone number listed in the advertisement came in slowly at first, but before long word started getting around, and Mary and Frank had to make the big decision to give up their jobs and work at the studio full time.

Frank now runs the exercise programmes and Mary has proved to be inspirational in motivating and encouraging their clients. The crash has been instrumental in giving others hope too! Mary has become close to her clients. At last she's found people who understand her, people who have suffered all their lives with a weight problem, as she has done. They can confide in her, and she in them, in a way they'd never been able to confide in anyone before. She understands them.   They have become her friends.   They go out together, join classes, play sports and go to restaurants— where every calorie is taken into account before they order their food! For the first time in her life she has an active and eventful social life and she revels in it! Their studio has become so well-known they've had to take on more staff and to put on more classes—but Frank and Mary remain informed about their clients progress—and should anyone regress heaven help them!

Val & Ben
Chapter 34

Val watched as Ben cradled their son in his arms and she felt a warm glow of love building inside her. It had been a long road for Ben to travel before he'd trusted her again. Not surprising really. She gave thanks that their love had been strong enough to survive as they tried to work things out.

She took in the sight of the two of them. Father and son. How lucky she'd been to be able to give him the son he'd always wanted. How could she ever have been unfaithful to him? She loved him so much it hurt! How could she have done that to him, and how could he have forgiven her?

She recalled the months after her return from hospital, when she was in so much pain, and even though he was hurting deeply inside, never stopped being anything other than a devoted husband. She really didn't deserve him. How she still dispised herself for putting him through that!

Now they were a family.

'Thank goodness you allowed me a second chance.'

Ben looked up, surprised by her words, but then he smiled and came to sit beside her, their baby between them, bonding them together.

'We found out a lot about each other Val, and perhaps even more about ourselves! I'd expected the family life I hadn't had with my own parents. In my ideal world I saw a large family that would always be there for me, offering me love and security: a far cry from my own upbringing! I wanted to put right all the things I saw as wrong with my parent's marriage, forgetting you may have different ideas. Each marriage is unique and the coming together of two very different people called for very different rules—and I hadn't seen that.'

Val reached up to stroke her husband's face and he turned to kiss her hand.

'And I was a selfish cow, only interested in holidays and fun. I wanted to replicate all the things I'd grown up with, far-away places, freedom, adventure. I knew one day I'd want to settle down and have babies but...,' she let her words trail away. 'Gradually I'd seen the man I'd married turning into a stick-in-the-mud and I wasn't ready for that. I was immature.'

'At least we've learnt to talk Val. We both had issues, and this young man will be taught to always voice his problems.'

Val had suffered a lot of back pain during her pregnancy but had felt it worthwhile once the tiny bawling little bundle of joy had been placed into her arms. She had questioned though if she'd be prepared to go through nine months of agony again. Having seen her pain Ben readily agreed with her. They had, after all, a healthy and happy son and they knew they should be thankful for that. However, she knew in her heart Ben was disappointed, and although they'd talked about it at length, her guilt still lingered in her mind and wouldn't go away. She felt constantly as if she were letting him down.

One evening, after Ben had arrived home from work and they'd settled the baby in his crib, Val poured two glasses of wine and took one across to Ben. She sat on the arm of his chair.

'What's this? A bit early for wine isn't it?' remarked Ben.

'I've been thinking about our future for some time Ben!' Val blurted out.

Ben looked startled not knowing what she was about to say.

'We know pregnancy can never be an option for me Ben—but what do you think about fostering? We always talked of having a large family, didn't we? Instead of having children of our own, what do you think about becoming parents to children who, through no fault of their own, need a family to look after them? There must be so many out there who need to be loved and nurtured? We've got enough love to go round, haven't we?'

Ben frowned. 'I'm not sure, let me think about it. We'd need to check with your doctors first to see if they think you'd be strong enough.'

'I've already done that. I knew I would be your first consideration. I do love you Ben.'

Soon they'd set the ball in motion and had looked into the pros and cons of fostering. It took a while to set it up as they had to go through a lot of red-tape—but they're now fully committed to their extended family and their home is always buzzing with happy laughter, loud music and occasionally some tears!

They find the hardest part is when one of their foster children is found a permanent home and has to leave them! However, they also know there are hundreds of other children out there waiting for their help and their love, and soon another little lost soul will come wandering in through their front door, looking frightened and confused. Yes, they have their problems too, but nothing they can't solve between them—and they see their life ahead, at least for the next few years, being full of Christmas trees and Santa's, laughter and love.

Danny & Lucinda
Chapter 35

Dan woke, with the sun streaming in through the bedroom windows. He lay for a moment feeling its warmth upon his face. He then threw back the covers, got out of bed and walked across to open the double doors, before going out onto the balcony. The sea glistened in the morning sunlight and he watched two ships on the horizon. He turned back to look at his sleeping wife, her hair straddled across her lovely face. As if knowing she was being watched she stirred and rolled over.

'Come on sleepy head,' he called, 'it's time to wake up. It's time to begin the first day of our married life.'

Danny and Lucinda's wedding had been beautiful, so full of youth and happiness, fun and warmth. Lucinda had looked radiant as she walked down the aisle and Danny couldn't believe how lucky he was. It hadn't been an enormous wedding, neither of them wanted that. They'd experienced enough notoriety to last them a lifetime.

They'd waited for Maggie to be released from prison before they'd tied the knot, determined she should experience their happiness too. It had been a long time for her to have something to smile about! Lucinda had gone to live with her mother for a short while once she'd been released, just long enough for her to learn to stand on her own two feet and to realise she was capable of living alone and didn't need to answer to a man any more, certainly not to a man like Brendon. She and Lucinda had relished the time they'd spent choosing outfits for the wedding, putting the past aside and looking forward to the future.

Danny had also learned lessons. He'd had to grow up very quickly and take on a great many responsibilities in a very short space of time. Falling in love had taken him along a difficult path, a path it would have been easier not to have travelled. However, with a background like his it became impossible to turn his back on something that felt so right. Once he'd experienced Brendon's wrath at the hospital, it would have been much easier to have walked away, long before the romance had a chance to get started; but Danny's upbringing wouldn't allow him to do that.

But that wasn't the only lesson he'd learnt. He had become conscious that the father he'd looked up to and admired, and modelled himself on for eighteen years, the father that had taught him to stand up for his beliefs, was himself fallible. This had come as a huge shock to the impressionable young Danny, making him determined never to be seduced by the lure of wealth or to forget his true values.

However, he also realised it wasn't only his father that had made mistakes. He'd made quite a few of his own. He'd been out of order holding back information about Brendon causing the accident and even though he'd done it with the best of intentions, it had been wrong and had helped no one. He now knew that even when it is uncomfortable, it's always best to tell the truth!

Watching what Lucinda's family had gone through had made them all, as a family, sit up and appreciate how lucky they were to have each other! Geoffrey and Jennifer Stokes had taken Lucinda to their hearts and weekends were now set aside for family whenever possible—family meals around the big table in the dining room, where they all talk for hours putting the world to rights!

It had been no surprise to anyone when Danny announced he was going to become a politician! What else? As he'd once reminded his father, it was the way he'd been brought up!

Danny and Lucinda, just like Tess and Daisy, Mary and Frank, Val and Ben, were all drawn together by need, a need for understanding, companionship, compassion and loyalty and out of that need love will flourish. Because of the crash, they'd all been exposed to some harsh realities, realities they had all managed to overcome.

Daisy
Chapter 36

One careless moment, a moment that was to change the lives of so many people, in so many ways. The bereaved, the injured, the onlookers, the hospital workers—none will forget that rainy September morning—a morning that began like any other and yet one that was to influence all their lives.

However, the final story must come from Daisy! Daisy, who little realised on the day her world fell apart, how life would pan out for her and what, with Tess's help, she would go on to achieve. She'd been a frightened little girl who'd found comfort in her own world of make-believe and imagination. Luckily, she'd found the one person capable of understanding how to allow that imagination to develop. Tess had been able to help channel those negative emotions, allowing Daisy to eventually turn herself into the world-class actress she has now become. Tess and Daisy adored each other. Their relationship was so very special because they'd both experienced loss and understood just how temporary life could be. Sadly, it couldn't last forever, and Daisy was left with one last letter to write:

'Dear Tess,

My last letter to you is to give thanks—thanks that you have been in my life—always there to show me the way! We came together when we both needed each other. Who needed who the most I'm still not quite sure. Perhaps our roles kept changing over the years. I was so relieved when, after you became ill, you agreed to come and live with us. I lost so much when my mum was killed in that car crash—just as you had lost part of yourself when Ellie had died. How lucky we were to find each other Tess!

My Tess. My Mom. My Life!'

From your loving daughter—Daisy. X'

Daisy allowed her hand to gently caress the bare mound of earth before her, and beneath her hand she felt some unknown force, magnet-like, holding her there. She closed her eyes, connecting with it and felt the sun warm about her shoulders, like a comforting hug, telling her that all would be well. Her heightened senses took in the sound of birdsong, their sweet trills bringing her back into her living world and breaking the connection.

Daisy kissed the letter, and as she did a teardrop fell onto the paper, before she hugged it to her heart. She then placed it between the twelve blood-red roses that she'd brought with her to lie on Tess's grave—red roses that reminded her of the first time they had met on that fateful day, the day when her mother had died and the day that Tess had drunk tea from her grandmother's gold-rimmed china cups, decorated with red roses.

Daisy slowly and reluctantly rose from her knees and walked away from Tess's grave, with tears in her eyes and a heavy grief-stricken heart. As she looked up she saw two birds circling above her. She stopped and watched them as they spiralled higher and higher, until they joined together to become no more than a speck in the clear blue sky. Daisy smiled, her heart brimming over with love and loss, and she spoke with less than a whisper:

'Fly free with Ellie Tess, fly free!'

THE END

Acknowledgements

To Mat Nunn and Kathryn Azarpay
my heartfelt thanks for guiding me
on this, my 'new beginning'.

15986548R00139

Printed in Great Britain
by Amazon